Murd

at the
Christmas Market

A Lady Marjorie Snellthorpe Mystery
Book 3

Dawn Brookes

Murder at the Christmas Market

A Lady Marjorie Snellthorpe Mystery

Dawn Brookes

Oakwood Publishing

Paperback Edition 2022
Paperback ISBN: 978-1-913065-72-0
Copyright © DAWN BROOKES 2022
Cover Images adapted from Adobe Stock Images:
Cover Design: John and Janet

Chapter 1

It was only for a few nights, Marjorie told herself after scanning the final guest bedroom. She was satisfied that they were prepared for the houseguests.

The doorbell rang, but it didn't just ring once; it rang constantly. There was nothing more irritating than a person repeatedly ringing a doorbell without giving the building's occupants time to answer.

It can't be Edna, her train's not due in until lunchtime and Horace promised to pick her up.

The bell stopped momentarily, but rang again while Marjorie crossed the gallery on the first floor. She took the main staircase down to the ground floor, noticing that even the banisters had been polished. Her housekeeper had done an excellent job.

"All right, I'm coming." Marjorie heard Jeremy before seeing him striding towards the front door. "Where's your housekeeper?" he snapped, seeing her descending the stairs.

Hiding, if she's got any sense, Marjorie thought, but answered, "She's been busy preparing rooms for *your* guests. I don't know how I let you talk me into this, Jeremy. It really is too much, and if all your business colleagues are going to be as impatient as the whoever that is outside, you can find alternative arrangements." Marjorie felt annoyance rising in her chest when the bell rang yet again. Her son had assured her people wouldn't be arriving until later.

Jeremy swatted away her protest with a wave of the hand, using the other to open the door with such force it almost hit the wall. A harsh and chilly wind drove into the hallway, causing Jeremy to almost lose his footing.

"Oh, it's you, Marcus," he said.

The man called Marcus pressed one more time with his trigger finger before barking, "This doorbell doesn't work. I've been standing here for ages."

Another loud ding-dong, ding-dong chime rang through the hallway.

Marjorie glared from behind Jeremy. "As you can hear, the bell is working, so if you could remove your finger?" she replied.

"Well, I couldn't hear it from outside."

That's because doorbells are meant to be heard inside, thought Marjorie.

"Let me introduce you to my mother," said Jeremy, letting the man in and pushing the door closed against the resistant gale blowing outside.

Marjorie felt her forehead wrinkle with confusion. Who was this Marcus person? She scanned the guest list she had memorised in her head, but didn't recall anyone going by that name.

We have allocated all the spare rooms.

Jeremy took the man's overcoat and hung it on the coatrack in the hallway. Marcus was around six foot and wore a navy-blue pinstripe suit with matching tie. His dyed black hair, parted in the centre, hung down over his eyebrows.

"Mother, this is Marcus Singleton, our chief negotiator. Marcus, this is my mother, Lady Marjorie Snellthorpe."

Chief negotiator since when? Marjorie took the man's outstretched hand, noticing long, stubby fingers which felt cold to the touch.

"How do you do?" she said.

"Very well, thank you. It's a pleasure to meet you, Lady Snellthorpe." Whilst his tone was warm, his eyes quickly moved away from her, greedily scanning the hallway in a way which made her feel uncomfortable. "This is very grand. It will do nicely, Jeremy. Shall we look around?"

Marcus Singleton had only been through the door a few minutes and he was already grating on Marjorie's frayed nerves.

Jeremy cleared his throat. "Perhaps you'd like a drink first."

"It's a bit early in the day for me," said Marcus.

"There will be a tray of tea and coffee in the sitting room," Marjorie said, rolling her eyes towards Jeremy.

"Follow me." Marjorie's son led them towards the large oak door behind the stairs. "Through there," he said, allowing Marcus to pass ahead.

"His name's not on the list," Marjorie hissed at Jeremy as they followed.

Jeremy spoke loud enough for Marcus to hear. "Marcus isn't staying overnight, Mother. He's heading up the business negotiations, though, so he will join you and our guests for meals and outings. I asked him to come early because he wants to get to know the lie of the land and make sure the kitchen staff are well prepared."

Marjorie's temper was fraying even more than her nerves. She stopped dead in her tracks, not knowing which of Jeremy's revelations to address first. Marcus was helping himself to coffee from the pot.

She took Jeremy to one side. "I don't need any of your friends – or rather, employees – checking on my staff. Thank you."

Jeremy lowered his voice. "They're not your staff, Mother. You told me you needed more help, which is why I arranged for a cook and extra hands to help with serving and cleaning for the week. I could have outsourced the cooking, but you wanted the food prepared here. If you didn't want any interference, you should have let me bring in outside catering."

"And have one of your guests end up with food poisoning! At least if the food is prepared here, I know where it comes from. This is my house and my rules, Jeremy. But if you don't like it, there's still time for you to find an alternative."

Jeremy sighed, putting a reassuring hand on her shoulder. "It'll be all right, Mother. I promise. Marcus just wants to meet people, that's all."

"If you say so," she conceded. Marjorie should have refused when he press-ganged her into hosting his potential new suppliers the week before Christmas. She was feeling fractious under the strain. Jeremy left her, satisfied he'd won, and helped himself to a coffee.

She heard the wretched ding-dong of the doorbell again. *I need to get a more calming chime, perhaps even a tune*, Marjorie told herself. She poked her head into the hallway and saw Gina heading to the door, so she joined Jeremy and Marcus Singleton. The latter was staring at her paintings.

"Is that an original?" Marcus had his eyes on an oil painting.

"Yes, it is. It's by an American artist called Thomas Kinkade. He died far too young. Do you like art, Mr Singleton?"

"Indeed, I do. I have quite a collection myself." Marcus had become animated and was examining the signature in the bottom right-hand corner.

Marjorie owned several original paintings, some of which had been handed down from her late husband's family and some she had purchased herself over the years. She wondered if Marcus Singleton's interest in art was just for show, but felt unkind thinking it. One thing was certain: she would have to keep this man away from Edna. He was likely to bring out the worst in her cousin-in-law, who could spot a fake from ten miles away.

There she was again: judging a man she'd only just met. It didn't bode well for the rest of the week. She chastised herself once more over the reason she had agreed to host Jeremy's business friends.

Once polite conversation had dried up, Marjorie interrupted the men's business chat. "My friends will be arriving shortly; would you like me to show you around now, Mr Singleton?" Marjorie hoped the earlier ring of the doorbell had been the cook who would be standing in for her own cook Gloria for the next five days.

"That would be spiffing," Marcus said.

Marjorie raised an eyebrow towards her son, who just shrugged.

"Perhaps you would like to follow me, then?" Marjorie led them back into the hallway and began the tour in the library, as it was closest to the sitting room.

"Who reads all these books?" Marcus sniffed.

"My late husband was an avid reader, Mr Singleton. I enjoy a good book myself, but I could never compete with his desire for a classic."

"Hmm." Marcus sniffed again before sneezing. "Shall we move on?"

"I take it you're less interested in reading than you are in art?" Marjorie was grateful this rude man, who was becoming more irritating by the minute, wouldn't be staying in her home.

"I don't see the point of keeping them; too much dust, if you ask me." He sneezed again for effect. "Let's get on, shall we?"

"Of course," said Jeremy. "Come on, Mother, there's nothing to see in here."

Why did Jeremy pander to such people? "Very well."

Marjorie inhaled a calming breath before continuing the impromptu tour of her home. They crossed the main hall, passing the sitting room where they'd had tea, and moved into the centre of the house.

"There's a toilet under the stairs over there and more conveniences in an annexe off the kitchen." She waved a hand in the first facility's direction and passed her study, which she used more as a reading room these days, without opening the door. A burst of sunlight shone through the ornate windows over the stairs. Marjorie often paused halfway down the stairs to take in the grand view of the front gardens, but she had no intention of taking Marcus further than the ground floor. "It appears to have stopped raining."

Marjorie led the way into the large banqueting room where she and Ralph used to entertain his business guests. The mahogany dining table, which had been freshly polished, could extend almost the length of the room. The staff would lay it ready for dinner this evening, but there would be no need to extend it. Marjorie rarely ate in this room, but she couldn't bring herself to change it around. The dining space had been one reason she and her late husband Ralph had bought the house, it being so suited to entertaining.

The doors adjoining the banqueting room were closed. Jeremy slid one of them open to reveal the more spacious and formal sitting room with settees and chairs surrounding a large open fireplace and other seating scattered around. Another room Ralph had used frequently when holding charity balls or conducting business meetings.

Marcus marched around the room with his nose in the air. Thankfully, with no sniffing or sneezing.

"This room will do nicely, Jeremy. We can hold separate discussions. We'll need to rearrange some of the furniture…"

Marjorie felt her jaw tighten, but said nothing.

"… but yes," the bumptious man continued, "this is where we'll conduct most of our business."

Jeremy cleared his throat, avoiding eye contact with his mother. "I'm sure we can accommodate."

"I'll leave you gentlemen to your plans." Marjorie pursed her lips and made towards the door.

"I still need to meet the staff," Marcus called after her.

Forcing a smile, Marjorie agreed, opening another door off the large sitting room which took them back into the hallway.

"Follow me. I'll introduce you to my housekeeper and cook, although the latter is leaving for her holiday today." Marjorie sighed at the reminder of how inconvenient Jeremy's imposition was. "She's visiting family for the Christmas break."

Marcus Singleton stopped in his tracks, glaring at Jeremy.

"But you have a replacement, Mother." Jeremy's tone was sharp. "There's nothing to worry about, the temp comes highly recommended. I sourced her myself."

Without meeting the woman. Marjorie hoped she hadn't said that out loud. "I heard the doorbell earlier, so I assume she's arrived," she said instead. "The staff will be very busy, Mr Singleton, so please don't keep them too long."

"I didn't hear any doorbell," Jeremy moaned, shooting his mother a worried look. What hold over her son did this Marcus have? Marjorie was feeling more anxious with each step towards the kitchen.

The door swung open.

"Ah, Mrs Ratton, I'm pleased we've—"

Marjorie didn't have time to finish the sentence. She noticed her housekeeper's eyes widen just before hearing the clattering of broken crockery as the tray Gina Ratton had been holding hit the floor.

"I... I... I'll get something to clean that up."

Marjorie had never seen her usually calm and efficient housekeeper so flustered. She tried giving a reassuring smile, but Gina scurried back to the kitchen.

"What's got into her?" Jeremy fumed, wiping a few drops of tea from his trousers. He turned to Marcus Singleton. Marcus's eyes bulged as he stared at the kitchen door, his face bright red and a pulse throbbing in his forehead.

"I'm sorry about that, Marcus. Perhaps we can meet the staff later."

"That might be a good idea. We'll leave you to deal with your staff, Lady Snellthorpe." Marcus swivelled on his heels and marched back towards the sitting room with Jeremy in hot pursuit.

Chapter 2

Gina was standing by the Belfast sink, gripping the counter tops on each side as she stared out into Marjorie's garden, her shoulders slumped. Marjorie walked into the kitchen and placed a hand lightly on her housekeeper's arm. Gina flinched slightly at Marjorie's touch.

"Are you all right, my dear?" Marjorie asked gently.

"I'm so sorry, Marjorie," Gina's voice was croaky. "I should never have been this clumsy." She wrung her hands but straightened up. Tears gathered in her eyes, which she blinked away. Her cheeks looked hollow and the words, "I'm sorry," became a repeated gurgle in her throat.

Gina ran into the scullery off the annexe, banging the door open and closed behind her. Marjorie could hear the clanging of pots and pans coming from within. The house was growing disturbingly manic. What had got into her housekeeper? She wasn't the kind of woman to behave in this way. Did she know Marcus Singleton? Or was it the same stress building up that Marjorie had been feeling, catching up with her? She heard another bang in the scullery. Now wasn't the time to pry.

"What happened outside?" Elsa, Marjorie's housemaid, flung the kitchen door open before pausing. "Oh, sorry, Marjorie, I didn't see you there."

Another bash came from the scullery. "Gina's had an accident. I think it's shaken her up. Perhaps you would be so kind as to give her a hand?"

The keen-eyed Elsa hid her surprise. "She's had a lot on her plate with all the guests arriving today," she explained. "We all have."

Don't I know it? thought Marjorie. "I'll make it up to you, I promise," she said. "Do you know where Gloria is?"

"She's showing that new cook around." Marjorie caught a hint of disapproval in her housemaid's tone. None of them liked the thought of having a stranger catering for houseguests, least of all Marjorie, but it couldn't be helped.

"It's only for five days."

"But…" Elsa hesitated.

Marjorie felt herself tense. "But what?" There was no time to wait for the reply as the doorbell chimed its ding-dong sound again. "Don't worry, I'll get it. I expect it will be my friends Horace and Frederick with Edna, who you met when she stayed here." Marjorie didn't miss the smirk on Elsa's face. "Horace kindly offered to collect them from the station. It's handy them both arriving via King's Cross.

"Do you think we could have fresh tea and coffee sent to the sitting room when you have a minute? My son and his negotiator have used the drinks you kindly put out for my friends' arrival. There's no rush." Marjorie puckered her nose as she turned to go. "There's a strange smell down here—"

Another crash came from the scullery. Marjorie's heart lurched.

"Don't worry, Lady Marjorie. I'll get the mess cleared up, and then I'll see to your tray. Gloria will be back any minute now."

Marjorie hesitated, but there was no time to do anything but answer the door. "Thank you," she said, fearing her housekeeper might not be the only person to fall apart over the next five days.

On reaching the front door, Marjorie was thankful that whoever was on the other side had more patience than Marcus Singleton. She pulled it open cautiously, not wishing to be blown over, but the wind that had followed Marcus appeared to have died down. Marjorie was delighted to see Frederick's twinkling grey eyes smiling up at her from the second step.

"Am I pleased to see you," she said, adding quickly, "and the others, of course."

Horace was unloading luggage from his car parked on the gravel driveway in front of the house. Edna was overseeing.

"Careful with that one, it's got breakables inside."

Marjorie grinned. Even Edna's brash ways would be welcome this week. All was well with her world again. Frederick remained on the doorstep, carrying a holdall.

"It's good to see you, Marjorie. Thanks for the invite."

"Thank you for coming. I do hope I haven't disrupted your Christmas plans."

"Not at all. I think the kids were relieved at not having to invite me. They can see the in-laws this year." He laughed.

"Where are my manners? Do come inside. I think those two might be a while." Edna and Horace appeared to be having a private catchup and were in no hurry to join them.

Frederick hesitated. "Should I help them?"

"Horace seems to have things in order."

The boot slammed as Frederick took tentative steps into the hallway. "Have your other guests arrived?"

Marjorie had forgotten what a simple life Frederick led and how he was often intimidated by wealth. "No. It's just my son at the moment, along with his negotiator or some such thing. The business guests aren't arriving until late this afternoon. Then I'm afraid the mêlée will begin." She hadn't the heart to tell him it already had. "I really appreciate this, you know."

Fredrick's cheeks flushed.

"Hello, Marge." Marjorie's cousin-in-law showed no such bashfulness. Edna Parkinton wrapped her arms around Marjorie before she could step away. Breathless from the near smothering, she wrestled herself free.

"It's good to see you, Edna, and you, Horace. Thank you so much for coming."

Horace took Marjorie's hand and kissed it. "Where's the bedlam, then?"

"Coming later. I wanted you all here before they arrive. That way you can help me prepare. I haven't entertained this many people for years."

"Don't you worry, Marge. We'll keep them in line," Edna said.

"Thank you. I would be grateful." Marjorie couldn't believe how happy she was at seeing the familiar faces of her three friends. It had only been a few months since they were on holiday in the Scottish Highlands, but if she was honest, she missed them. The only plus side to Jeremy's blasted business meetings was that they had given her the opportunity to invite them all to stay. She had feared they might decline her offer, but was delighted when they agreed to help.

"Would you like coffee before I show you to your rooms?"

"That would be nice. I can never drink the stuff they serve on trains," said Frederick.

"Me neither. It's like dishwater or mud," Edna agreed. "Lead the way, Marge."

"You know the way," said Marjorie, noticing for the first time Edna's new wig when she removed her headscarf.

"There's no need to gawp. I thought I'd go for a sixties look." Edna patted the mop atop her head. "There are advantages to having alopecia, you know."

"Uh, well, you have certainly achieved the sixties style." Edna's black beehive loomed upwards, reminding Marjorie of a tower. "I'm short enough without you wearing a skyscraper," she said, laughing. "Please hang your coats on the pegs. If you would like to take them up to your rooms later, you may."

Marjorie watched closely while Edna removed her coat, releasing a breath she hadn't realised she was holding, relieved to see that her cousin-in-law hadn't added the sixties miniskirt to the new appearance. Horace looked dapper in a beige suit while Frederick had donned a check suit with his usual clashing but colourful striped tie.

"You look lovely," Horace whispered to Edna, just loud enough for the others to hear. "As do you, Marjorie."

"Thank you. Now, before we go into the small sitting room…" Marjorie ignored the splutter from Edna, who had suggested it might be time for Marjorie to downsize, "…my son Jeremy is here with a man called Marcus Singleton. He's brusque."

"Your son or Singleton?" Horace asked.

Well, both, actually, thought Marjorie, but said, "Marcus. But don't worry, it appears he's just a day visitor, here to negotiate whatever deal Jeremy is concocting."

"I thought you looked a bit peaky," said Edna. "We'll deal with him, won't we, boys?"

"Please don't. I'd rather just get this whole thing over with. I was hoping Jeremy would lock the guests in meetings all day, but he let slip they might expect outings of some kind."

"Leave that one to me, Marjorie. I've got Faith on standby," said Horace.

"Faith Weathers?" Edna arched an eyebrow.

"Yes. We keep in touch."

"Do you now?" Edna pouted.

"Not like that. She's done a few private jobs for the firm when my sons have international guests. When Marjorie mentioned this shindig, I asked her what her plans were, knowing what it can be like hosting guests in London. It turns out she'll be staying with her mother not too far from here. I think she'll be glad of an excuse to get out. Her mother's a bit of a stickler for routine. Not to mention she cramps Faith's style."

Marjorie brightened up. "Now you mention it, Faith would be a perfect fit if they are expecting formal tours rather than wanting to go off exploring by themselves. I'll see if I can ask Jeremy what he meant by outings."

"Not meaning to be rude, Marge, and as nice as it is, but are we going to be standing in this hallway all day? I'm parched."

"Of course not, Edna. Follow me. I can see Elsa with tea and coffee now."

Frederick raised a quizzical eyebrow, which Edna picked up on. "Elsa's the maid, Mrs Ratton's the housekeeper and Gloria's the cook; an excellent cook at that. And if you see a bloke washing a Rolls or a Bentley, that's Johnson, the chauffeur."

For once, Edna sounded more sarcastic than resentful, which was progress. Edna's resentment at her late father being disinherited caused occasional friction between the two women.

Elsa came out of the sitting room when they got there, her face lighting up when she set eyes on Edna.

"Hello, Mrs Parkinton."

"Edna to you, Elsa. These are the fellas, Horace and Fred."

Frederick! Marjorie gritted her teeth, hoping Edna wouldn't get under her skin after what had been a promising start.

"Nice to meet you," said Elsa, nodding at the two men.

"And you, Elsa," said Horace, holding out his hand.

Once the handshaking was done, Elsa looked at Marjorie. "Jeremy's in there." She nodded towards the sitting room. "I've left a tray. There's tea, coffee and hot water in case anyone wants fruit tea or anything. And I've done a small pot of Earl Grey tea for you, Marjorie. If it's okay with you, I'll grab an early lunch in the library."

Unlike Marcus Singleton, Elsa loved reading and spent most of her breaks during the winter in the library, with either one of her own books, or one belonging to the house.

"That's fine, thank you, Elsa. Is everything all right in the kitchen?"

"I think so. On the way here, I bumped into a man I've not met before; it might be the one you mentioned 'cos there's no-one with Jeremy. I asked if he was lost, but he said he was on his way to talk to the new cook and the housekeeper."

"Please, go through," Marjorie said to her friends. "I have something to attend to." She felt eyes boring into the back of her head as she forced her ageing legs to hurry towards the kitchen.

Chapter 3

The exertion caused Marjorie to pause for a breath before turning the corner to the kitchen. She stopped in her tracks when she heard a low-pitched snarling, interspersed with pants and guttural growls.

She took a moment to recover, her breath catching in her throat when she saw what was happening. Marcus Singleton had his back to the wall. A monster of a dog stood as if on guard, baring huge teeth, growling menacingly at him. The brown and black animal wore a dark-brown leather collar around its neck. Its eyes travelled from Marcus's face to his hands, as if daring him to move.

On realising she was in no danger herself, Marjorie suppressed the urge to laugh. Instead, she smiled inwardly at the comical sight.

"Don't just stand there. Call your blasted dog off." Marcus's raised voice prompted the beast's growl to get louder and deeper. With hackles raised on the back of its neck and ears twitching, it inched forwards towards him.

Marcus whimpered; his eyes pleaded with Marjorie.

"I'm afraid the animal doesn't belong to me or anyone in the household. I don't know where it came from."

The tension became palpable. Marcus turned pale, but gritted his teeth. He spoke carefully, mumbling lest he cause the dog to attack.

"I don't care where it came from. Please call it away."

"Come here, dog," Marjorie spoke evenly, at which the animal left its prey, putting its tongue out and moving to stand in front of her with big brown eyes looking at her as if butter wouldn't melt. "There, there. Do you know how to sit?" She patted the dog's head as it immediately obeyed. Its fur felt silky smooth. "I think that explains the smell."

"What smell?" Marcus snapped, raising his voice. It was easy for him to be brave now the dog had released him, but it gave a low warning growl.

"I thought I could smell something odd in the kitchen earlier, that's all. It was obviously a dog." The dog growled at Marcus again when he opened and closed his mouth. "I suggest you keep your voice down, Mr Singleton. You're upsetting it. What are you doing here, anyway?"

"I told you earlier, I needed to meet the staff and I, erm… wanted to make sure there wouldn't be any more mishaps from your blundering housekeeper."

Marjorie wished she'd left the dog where it was. "May I remind you, Mr Singleton, that you are a guest in my home and my staff are not your concern. Mrs Ratton is an exceptional housekeeper and a dear friend, and I would ask you to refrain from upsetting or insulting her in any way."

"Fine. Well, I've had a word, anyway. I expect she'll get things right from now on." Marjorie felt he would have barged past her had it not been for another warning growl from her newfound protector. Instead, he sidled past, pacing along the wall before scampering away.

Marjorie released the laughter that had been welling up from her stomach before staring hard after Marcus Singleton. "Good riddance," she muttered, looking once more into the brown doe eyes of the enormous beast. "I can see you have good instincts. Now, what's your name?" Marjorie leaned down to get a closer look at the name tag hanging from the collar. "Hmm, that fits. Now, come along, let's find out who you belong to and what chaos that wretched man left in his wake."

Marjorie strode towards the kitchen, but couldn't help feeling she was being watched. She turned to find a tall, muscular woman wearing jeans and a tie-dye top appearing out of nowhere. The woman must have been hiding while watching the Marcus versus dog incident.

"I see you've met Hercules," she said, with a wide grin on her face.

"Indeed I have, but I haven't had the pleasure of meeting his owner, whom I assume is you." Marjorie watched Hercules smothering the tall woman in affectionate licks when she bent down to greet him. Her black hair, tied back in a ponytail, was as silky smooth as that of her dog.

"Good boy, Hercules," she said before offering a hand to Marjorie. "I'm Sally Sutherland; your cook for as long as you need."

Marjorie took the hand, which was warm and slightly rough. Sally's fingers were long and slender. The nails were neatly trimmed, and the anatomical snuffbox between the thumb and forefinger was decorated with a small tattoo of a rose.

"Marjorie Snellthorpe, how do you do? We're so pleased you could come at such short notice, Ms Sutherland. I believe my son Jeremy has been your primary contact. He mentioned nothing about a dog, though."

"Please call me Sally, or I'll think I'm in trouble. I'm sorry about Hercules being here. My parents were going to look after him, but my dad likes to think he's the alpha male, so they didn't get on."

Marjorie chortled, warming to the new cook. Sally was around the same age as Elsa, perhaps younger, and had a Birmingham accent.

"He's just encountered another alpha male, as you put it, but I think you already know about that."

Sally frowned. "Guilty. I would have intervened if that man had been in any real danger. He tried to nudge Hercules out of the way and got what he deserved, in my opinion."

"Do you always speak so frankly?" The cook's outburst surprised Marjorie. "Or do you already know Mr Singleton?" *The plot thickens,* she thought.

"Not always. I met him briefly, and thought he was in charge from the way he went on, but Gloria said she'd never seen him before. By the way, Gloria said to tell you goodbye. She didn't want to interrupt while you were with your friends."

Marjorie scrutinised Sally Sutherland. Intelligent dark-green eyes. She seemed strangely familiar, but they hadn't met before. Marjorie would remember if they had.

"Thank you. Did Gloria show you where everything is?"

"Yeah. She and Gina also showed me to my room on the second floor. I hope you don't mind Hercules bunking in with me."

"Do I have a choice?" Marjorie asked.

Sally shrugged. "Not if you want your guests fed."

The two women laughed. "I can see we'll get along just fine, Sally. I'm pleased you've already met Gina. Did you meet Elsa?"

"We did, didn't we, Hercules? Nice woman, but I don't think she likes dogs."

The dog gave an adoring pant, an enormous pink tongue hanging out. He was almost smiling.

"I'm sure he's capable of worming his way into her good books. What kind of dog is he?"

"A Rottweiler, but don't let that put you off. He's a big softie."

"Unless he meets alpha males." Marjorie chuckled. "I expect Gloria told you there would be ten for dinner, but Mr Singleton will also join us for meals. I hope that won't be a problem?"

"Not at all, as long as he stays away from Hercules. What about the staff?"

"Gina stays for lunch, but goes home each night. Elsa brings her own food with her – she's a fussy eater. You can, of course, help yourself to whatever you like. We don't have any dog food, so I hope you've brought some of your own."

"Hercules only eats steak."

Marjorie's eyes widened.

"I'm just kidding, Lady Marjorie. Yes, I've brought dog food, and plenty of it; he likes his food. We'll be fine. Gloria left sandwiches already prepared for today's lunch and baked a tonne of cakes in case any of your guests were hungry before dinner. How many are there for lunch?"

"Six if no-one arrives early. Jeremy has arranged for some agency workers to serve food at dinner and breakfast and to help keep the rooms neat and tidy. You can manage them around mealtimes and Gina will tell them what to do in-between. I'm rather hoping the guests will be out for luncheons, but they may need packed food if that's not too much trouble. My son mentioned outings. If they're not out, I'm sure they will be happy with finger food."

"That all sounds brilliant. Elsa said she would help me carry up lunch."

"That's good. Oh, I forgot to mention, one houseguest is a vegetarian."

"Gloria gave me the list. I was going to ask you about that. Is Mrs Beider vegan or vegetarian?"

"Is there a difference?"

"Yep, but leave it with me. I'll check with her later and ensure she gets a wonderful selection of food. Your fridge and freezer are well stocked, and Gloria's left plenty of winter vegetables for me to play with."

"That's settled, then. Do you happen to know where Gina is?"

"She said she was going out for a walk the last time I saw her."

"I see. Well, thank you, Sally. I hope you – and Hercules – enjoy your temporary stay with us. Would you mind bringing lunch to the small dining room in about half an hour? Elsa will show you where it is."

"Consider it done, Lady Marjorie."

"If I'm going to call you Sally, you'll need to call me Marjorie. All the staff do." Marjorie wondered if Sally Sutherland would change out of her faded jeans and tie-dye shirt before getting to work, but somehow imagined she wouldn't. Sally gave the impression of being a free spirit who would do things her way. And so long as that didn't cause any friction in her household, Marjorie would make allowances. "Would you mind keeping Hercules away from the guests? Some people don't like dogs."

"I've set him up a bed in the scullery. Don't worry. He knows the rules and will stay out of the kitchen when I'm preparing food."

That's a relief, thought Marjorie, saying, "I'll leave you to get on then. Please let me or Jeremy know if there's anything else you need."

"Thanks, I will. Right, Hercules… bed!"

It impressed Marjorie when the dog went straight through the open door into the annexe hallway and turned left into the scullery. She herself left in the opposite direction and headed back towards the sitting room.

"I need a cup of Earl Grey tea," she said out loud, pondering what had got into Gina. Perhaps she could ask Jeremy to hold his meetings somewhere else, but she already knew what the answer to that would be.

Chapter 4

"There you are, Marge. I know this is a big house, but surely you know your way around it well enough not to get lost."

Ignoring Edna's jibe, Marjorie said, "I'm sorry to have kept you, but I was meeting the temporary cook. My cook had longstanding plans to visit family with her husband and I couldn't keep her from them. Jeremy has arranged for someone to stand in, along with external waiting staff who will serve meals and attend to rooms."

Edna opened and closed her mouth, giving Marjorie some hope that she was at least going to try to rein herself in.

"Can I pour you some tea, Marjorie?" Horace asked, giving Edna a warning look at the same time.

"I'd love a cup of Earl Grey. It should be in the small teapot."

Horace snorted, his merry eyes looking at Edna before returning to Marjorie. "Yes, Edna discovered it by mistake. There's enough left for you."

Marjorie wondered whether Edna ever listened to anything. Elsa had clearly told them about her tea before they went into the sitting room.

"I don't know how you drink that stuff, Marge; it tastes like cheap perfume."

"The taste and smell come from bergamot oil and that's precisely what I like about it." Marjorie lowered her voice. "I assume you met Jeremy and Marcus Singleton." She couldn't help frowning at the mention of the latter's name. "Where are they?"

"We only saw Singleton briefly, but Jeremy was friendly. The two of them left for a tête-à-tête," said Frederick.

"In your study," said Edna disapprovingly.

Marjorie frowned. At least Jeremy had removed the unpleasant man from her sitting room.

"And you weren't wrong about him, Marjorie," said Horace. "Singleton, that is. A most unpleasant fellow. When he came in, Jeremy hardly got out his introductions before being hauled away."

"I'm assuming he's new, because I haven't heard of him before today," said Marjorie.

"I know Jeremy can be abrupt at times, but his new employee is downright rude. He's also the leader of that duo, employee or not," Edna remarked.

"Oh dear," said Marjorie. "I don't quite know what's going on. Marcus Singleton doesn't appear to be the sort of man you would want in charge of buying negotiations, does he?"

"You'd be surprised," said Horace. "Sometimes it's the ruthless types who get the best results. Don't worry, Marjorie, I'm sure your son has his reasons for bringing Singleton here. Jeremy wasn't abrupt with us, despite what Edna says. He seems a good sort and he must be astute to oversee your late husband's business."

Marjorie wanted to say that it was through blood, not ability, that Jeremy was in charge of the firm. More importantly, it was the reason she kept a controlling interest. But she felt that would be disloyal.

Instead, she said, "Lunch should be served soon. I suggest we eat while we can. I don't know what the incoming guests will be like, but I believe we're going to need to keep our energy up."

"Jeremy told us he won't be around tomorrow. He and his wife are visiting a Lord and Lady Somebody or Other.

He said Singleton would be here all day to manage things," Horace added.

"I'll be surprised if you've got any guests left by the end of tomorrow, Marge," said Edna, cackling. "That's one way of getting out of playing hostess."

Marjorie felt her jaw tense; she was furious enough with her son for inviting a crowd of people to stay in her home the week before Christmas without him abandoning them. And now it appeared he felt it was okay to leave Marcus Singleton in charge.

"This is still my home, and I will decide what goes on in it. It's obvious we need to get ahead of the game. Horace, would you mind asking Faith whether she would be available and willing to arrange something for tomorrow? I'll pay her, of course."

"No problem. I'll do it now."

"That's the spirit, Marge," said Edna, taking her arm. "But can we come up with a plan of action over lunch? I'm starving."

Marjorie jerked her arm away, looking up at her generously proportioned cousin-in-law. "I don't know where you put it, Edna Parkinton. I'm sure you will have had a fried breakfast before you left home this morning."

"That was hours ago," said Edna. "You said it yourself: we need our sustenance."

"Quite right. Although I'm afraid it's just sandwiches for lunch, but there will be enough to satisfy your…" voracious went unsaid "…appetite." Marjorie found herself grinning appreciatively at Edna, pleased to have her friends beside her. She felt she was going to need them even more now she had met Marcus Singleton.

"If not, I can always ask Elsa to sneak down to the kitchen and rustle me something up while the temp's not looking."

"You will do no such thing," said Marjorie.

The black beehive bobbed down when Edna slapped Marjorie on the back. "Got you there, didn't I?" Edna and Horace emitted joint snorts and Marjorie finished her tea, feeling all would be well, especially if Faith agreed to step in and help. She left Horace to make the phone call and led the others to the dining room.

***

Sally Sutherland had been as efficient as her word and had already laid trays of sandwiches on the side table for them to help themselves from. Elsa was just finishing laying the table.

"How are things downstairs, Elsa?" asked Marjorie.

"Apart from Hercules, they're fine. Sally seems to have her head screwed on. She told me how Hercules got rid of—"

"Quite." Marjorie interrupted. Normally she would welcome Elsa's frankness, but her concerns currently lay elsewhere. She drew the housemaid to one side while Edna took a plate and started helping herself to food, soon joined by Horace. "How is Gina?"

"She seems rattled. I've never seen her like this. According to Sally, it's got something to do with that Mr Singleton."

"In what way?"

"She didn't say, and Gina ain't gonna tell us. But I reckon she's going to make herself invisible while that guy's in the house."

Marjorie would need to find the time to speak with her housekeeper and find out whether there was any truth to Elsa's theory. It was a worrying turn of events, and one she hadn't expected. As if it wasn't disruptive enough having houseguests without one of them appearing to be upsetting her most loyal employee.

"Perhaps Sally is mistaken," she said.

"Maybe," said Elsa, shrugging. "I hope so. Anyway, if Hercules keeps him from coming near the kitchen, it can stay."

Marjorie grinned. "I don't think either of us has any choice on the Hercules matter."

"I don't suppose we do, but I wouldn't have let that bloke past me if I'd known he was going to upset Gina. Can I get you anything else?"

Marjorie turned her head, noticing that Horace and Edna had almost emptied the sandwich trays. Frederick was holding an empty plate, hovering to wait for her.

"Perhaps some more sandwiches, if there are any left. Could you take a tray through to Jeremy and Mr Singleton, please?"

"Already done. They were deep in conversation when I delivered them, so I don't think they'll bother you for a while."

Excellent, thought Marjorie. "Thank you, Elsa." She took another look over at Edna, who was devouring the sandwiches. "Would you also bring up one of the cakes Sally mentioned?"

Elsa laughed. "I'm on it," she said, winking.

Marjorie was still smiling at her housemaid's guileless honesty when she joined Frederick.

"If you're hungry, there are more sandwiches on the way," she said.

"Don't worry about me. I don't eat all that much."

Looking at his slim waist, Marjorie could believe it. He was the sort of man who needed feeding up. Once they had helped themselves to what was left of the food, they joined Edna and Horace, who were still enjoying each other's company.

"What was Elsa on about? Who the heck's Hercules?" Edna asked when Marjorie sat down.

"You have the uncanny ability to be selectively deaf on certain occasions and yet listen to two conversations at the same time on others."

"Just remember that the next time you complain about me behind my back," said Edna.

"I would only ever complain to your face," countered Marjorie.

"Go on, then. Who's this man Hercules, and when can I meet him?" Edna pressed.

"Hercules is the cook's dog."

"A dog! In your house? Now that I must see. Marge don't like dogs," Edna explained to Horace and Frederick.

"I'll have you know I have no problem with dogs. Remember my dear friend Rachel and her husband have a dog? And Hercules and I got on very well actually," said Marjorie, noticing Frederick's dancing eyes looking at her.

"That's a funny name for a dog," said Horace. "I expect someone's overcompensating and it's a Chihuahua."

"He's a Rottweiler, as a matter of fact," said Marjorie.

"Blimey," said Edna. "They're gigantic beasts. Did you know she was bringing a big dog?"

"No, I didn't. I encountered Hercules cornering Marcus Singleton while his owner, I'm almost certain, was hiding and enjoying the spectacle. I fear Marcus has already upset the staff."

"Never upset them that does the work," said Edna.

"An interesting way of putting it," said Marjorie, "but I agree with the sentiment."

"It's never dull spending time with you, Marjorie," said Horace with a low-toned guffaw.

Edna's eyes widened. "Sounds like your new cook can handle herself if she set her dog on him."

"I hardly think she set the dog on him on purpose."

Edna raised an eyebrow. "If you say so, Marge. Nevertheless, I hope it will not be cornering any of your other guests, and especially not me. I don't mind dogs, but some of these big ones can be unpredictable."

"As can some humans," said Frederick. "At least it's not the Loch Ness Monster," he added, grinning.

Edna had been terrified during their last holiday together that Nessie would emerge from Loch Ness, close to where they were staying. It had surprised them all to discover she had an irrational fear of the legendary beast.

"You watch the dog doesn't mistake your shiny head for a bone," Edna retorted.

Frederick's bald head wasn't something he was sensitive about, which was perhaps as well, because it was one of Edna's main teasing points. Thankfully, he was too much of a gentleman to point out that he wasn't the one wearing the wig, or the toupee, as in Horace's case.

"I'll keep it in mind," he replied.

"Come on, people. We need to stay focussed if we're going to help Marjorie out here," said Horace. "You'll be pleased to know that Faith's agreed to come over this evening and will offer to conduct a few tours while your guests are staying. Would you be able to give me a list of names and jobs so she can do her research?"

"That's wonderful. It will be good to see her again. And I'm pleased to hear she's as efficient as ever. I have the list in my study. I'll let you have it when I can get inside." Marjorie had grown fond of the tour guide who generally worked for Queen River and Land Tours.

"How many people are staying, Marge?"

"Five houseguests plus Marcus, who will be a day guest."

"Blimey! I thought we were going to be feeding the five thousand when you called in reinforcements."

Marjorie pursed her lips. "It may appear trivial to you, Edna, but I'm out of the way of entertaining strangers." Marjorie had known Edna would think she was overreacting, which was why she hadn't mentioned numbers before. Playing host had certainly felt overwhelming when Jeremy dropped it on her.

"I understand, Marjorie. As someone who has done it all in the past, I know it's not something I'd like dumped on me these days," Horace said.

"I thought you said you got Faith to help you with visitors," snapped Edna.

"On behalf of my sons. I'm in the fortunate position to be able to do as I please."

"Quite right," said Marjorie. "Please invite Faith to stay for dinner this evening if she's free. One more dinner guest won't hurt and it will give her an opportunity to meet the others on an equal footing. I don't want any of them lording it over her when she's doing me a favour."

Elsa brought in another tray of sandwiches. "Here you go," she said, looking at Edna. "Enjoy these and I'll bring up some cake."

Marjorie sat back in her chair, feeling more relaxed. All she had to do now was convince Jeremy to let Faith do what she did best.

Chapter 5

Jeremy stayed locked away in Marjorie's study, where he and Marcus had been for hours. The first guests were due to arrive at any minute. Edna and Horace had gone for a walk to get some fresh air before the *crowds,* as Edna sarcastically put it, arrived, and Frederick had fallen asleep while reading in the sitting room. Marjorie watched his chest moving rhythmically up and down, pleased he felt at home enough to nod off.

She and Frederick had become close over the months since their last holiday, speaking regularly on the telephone. Edna still teased her about the relationship, but she was wasting her time. Marjorie had decided their friendship would remain platonic. Friendship was more important than intimacy at her age, and she was happy to settle for that. Occasionally, she sensed Frederick would like something more, but she closed down any conversations that might veer in that direction. Looking at him now, she questioned whether it might be nice to have him around permanently.

Marjorie heard footsteps in the hall, which shook her mind away from any such notions. She hurried out of the sitting room and followed Elsa, who was carrying a tray to the study. She hung back until Jeremy answered the knock and Elsa went inside. Marjorie shadowed her, taking the opportunity to speak to her son while Elsa lay the tray down.

"Jeremy, the guests will arrive soon. Might I have a word?"

"Can it wait, Mother? Marcus and I are in the middle of something here."

Ignoring the dismissive waving of his hand, she said, "You mentioned guest outings when we spoke earlier. I just wanted you to know that I've invited Faith Weathers over for dinner this evening. She is going to arrange a tour for tomorrow and any other days when you are otherwise engaged." Marjorie spun around on her heels before Jeremy could come up with a riposte.

Elsa scurried after her. "Nicely done," she said before running off to the kitchen, no doubt to tell Sally and Gina the news.

Marjorie grinned, pleased to have got that over with. *I'd better tell Sally myself about the expanding dinner list.*

"Not so fast, Mother." Jeremy ran around her, stopping in front of her. She almost crashed into him. "You can't just spring things like this on us when we are conducting business."

"Jeremy, let me make something quite clear to you. When you asked, or rather pressured me into hosting your guests at short notice, you didn't mention outings and you didn't mention that you and Octavia would be swanning off to visit friends. And, might I add, you certainly said nothing about an employee I've never heard of who, in case you haven't noticed, is abrupt, verging on rude. Now, get out of my way, Jeremy, before I turn your guests away at the door."

"You wouldn't?"

"Don't test me." Marjorie felt herself trembling, but not with fear. It was anger. Anger at the fact she had been forced into a corner and that she might have to deal with the fallout of Jeremy's rude negotiator day in and day out.

"Please be reasonable. I prearranged dinner with Gregory and Cissie long before we got this new contract, for which we need to find parts suppliers so we can fulfil the orders."

Gregory and Cissie Fuller were two of Jeremy and his wife Octavia's pretentious friends. "My staff's holidays were also prearranged, but most of them have kindly changed those arrangements to accommodate you and your guests. If you will not be around tomorrow, then neither will your guests. It's not up for discussion, Jeremy. They will be under the care of Faith Weathers."

Jeremy held his palms up. "Okay, Mother. You win. Who is this Faith Weathers, anyway?"

"She's a very capable tour guide who has dropped everything to help this week run as smoothly as possible. Think of it this way: you're much more likely to conduct productive business with happy guests."

"I suppose you might be right, although when I mentioned outings, I didn't mean anything so formal. Still," he stroked his chin, "it could work. I'll ask Marcus, and if he agrees, you can go ahead, so long as he's happy to tag along."

Marjorie felt the tension rising in her chest. "If I were you, Jeremy, I would *tell* Marcus it's happening. I don't care whether he agrees or not. As to whether he wants to tag along, that's between the two of you. Now, if you'll excuse me, I need to speak to the cook you hired. The one you haven't even met."

Jeremy rubbed back his hair. "Why should I need to? Don't tell me she's no good… the agency promised me she is qualified and comes highly recommended."

"It's nothing like that. Sally Sutherland appears very capable. It's just—"

"Jeremy, we need to finish our business." Marcus's tall frame stood in the study doorway.

"Excuse me, Mother, I need to go. What is it you wanted to say?"

"It can keep," she replied, thinking now was not the time to ask her son why he sucked up to people like Lord and Lady Fuller and Marcus Singleton, but didn't give others the time of day. He had known Gina and Elsa for years, but he barely acknowledged them.

Marjorie sighed. She knew the answer. Her son was a snob who thought himself higher than he ought, despite opting not to use his title.

She plodded to the kitchen. The welcome sound of laughter rang out, and she found Elsa and Sally sitting at the square table, drinking tea. They hadn't heard her come in.

"I tell you, it's true," said Sally.

Marjorie didn't like to sneak up on the staff when they were relaxing, so she cleared her throat. Hercules poked his head from behind the scullery door in the corridor, but decided his mistress was in no danger, so he snorted and went back inside.

"That dog is so intelligent," Marjorie said.

Both women stood up, but she motioned them to sit down and joined them.

"We were just talking about Gloria. Sally said she told her to spike Mr Singleton's drink," said Elsa.

"That doesn't sound like the Gloria I know," said Marjorie.

"She didn't like the way he spoke to your housekeeper." Sally shot Elsa a warning look. "I could be exaggerating, though."

"I certainly hope so. There will be no spiking of anything in this house. Whatever impression any of us may have of Mr Singleton, he works for my son's company and has important business to attend to. I'll do my best to keep him and the other guests from troubling you, so please be patient."

"Elsa told me you're planning outings," said Sally. "Let me know if you want me to do pack-ups."

"That's a good idea. I'll check with the guests tonight." Marjorie turned her eyes on Elsa. "Please try to keep anything you overhear to yourself."

Elsa took a slurp from her mug of tea. "You can trust us, Lady Marjorie."

"Drop the 'Lady', Elsa. It's unnecessary."

"But I thought you might want me to use your title while you have company." The housemaid grinned.

"It doesn't sound right coming from your mouth. Anyway, the reason I've come along here is to let Sally know we have one extra for dinner. Faith Weathers is a friend and will be our tour guide. No special dietary requirements are necessary."

"Thanks for letting me know, although—"

"Elsa's already informed you."

"Yep, but thanks for doing it yourself." Sally flushed.

"I don't suppose either of you knows where I can find my elusive housekeeper?" The two women shook their heads. This was becoming exasperating. "Well, has she been here at all since this morning?"

Sally got up. "I'd better take Hercules for a walk before I make a start on dinner. Elsa said she'll do drinks when the first guests arrive."

After Sally had left and Marjorie was certain she and Hercules had gone out of the back door, she turned to Elsa.

"Well?"

"She had a headache and said to give you her apologies. She left early."

"Was this headache brought on by stress or by the gentleman in my study?"

"She didn't say, but I reckon the latter. I don't know whether they just got off on the wrong foot or whether she knows him from somewhere. Whatever it is, I've never seen her like this. She would never normally go home early without talking to you."

Marjorie felt a lump settle in her stomach. "I'll call her later to check she's all right. I'm sure Jeremy's troop can handle the guest rooms if she needs to take some time off and you can oversee them."

"Really? Thank you, Marjorie, I'll keep them in line."

"Mm," said Marjorie. *I'm not sure that's what I meant,* but she didn't want to dampen Elsa's enthusiasm. "Speaking of the troop, the extras will arrive at around six this evening. Could you show them where things are? They will only need to serve and clear away this evening, but we'll need them to help with rooms once the guests go out tomorrow."

"Cool," said Elsa. She looked as though she was about to say something else, but the doorbell rang.

"You finish your tea. If Jeremy hasn't answered by the time I get to the door, I'll deal with it." Marjorie strode towards the front of the house. "Let the mêlée begin."

Chapter 6

Faith was a big hit with Marge's guests. Edna watched them as they gathered around her, listening to her plans to take them to a Christmas market the following day. It was perhaps as well Horace had brought Faith in because Marcus Singleton would drive everyone bonkers if left to his own devices. Marge seemed particularly annoyed with him – not that it would be obvious to anyone else, but Edna felt she could read her cousin's moods.

"I knew Faith would go down well. When you're away on business, you need to have some relaxation." Horace had sidled up beside her and handed her a glass of champagne, before lowering his voice. "All's good so far. And no dead bodies; that's a plus."

Edna dug her elbow into his ribs, then said, "All she has to do now is keep that Marcus bloke out of Marge's hair."

"Indeed. I've been watching him and I agree with Marjorie. I can't imagine why her son put him in charge of what seem to be important negotiations. He just appears to get on everyone's nerves. Another thing I've noticed is that considering these people are here to compete for a contract, they're putting on a good show of being friendly."

"Maybe they're not that bothered about said contract," Edna replied.

Horace shook his head. "You don't travel the week before Christmas for something you're not interested in. I feel like we're taking part in a stage play with the last act yet to be revealed."

"Now you mention it, you could be right. But at least Faith's organisational skills will take some of the pressure off Marge. I'm worried about her. She doesn't seem herself."

"We can put that down to Marcus. Every time he goes near her, she stiffens."

"For a vain individual, you can be quite sensitive at times," said Edna.

"Touché." Horace clinked his glass against hers.

"That Marcus bloke upset Mrs Ratton." Elsa's voice broke through their conversation.

"You made me jump." Edna exchanged her empty glass for a full one from the tray Elsa was holding. "Has anyone ever told you that listening in to other people's conversations is rude?"

"It's what housemaids are best at," said Elsa, winking. Edna laughed. The housemaid had a habit of giving a naughty wink whenever she was up to something.

"I didn't have you down as an eavesdropper, but come on, then, spill the beans," Edna said. "How has Marcus Singleton managed to upset Marge's housekeeper?"

Elsa shrugged. "I don't know. I weren't there, but the new cook was, and she don't like him either."

"I don't think anyone does." Edna was thoughtful.

Horace nudged her. "That woman over there doesn't like him, that's for sure."

Edna followed Horace's eye line and observed the tall, busty woman they had been introduced to earlier, but whose name she couldn't recall. She and Marcus Singleton were having a heated discussion while standing at the edge of the room.

"What's that all about?"

"Business, I suppose; so much for them not caring," said Horace. "She's rather attractive, don't you think?"

Edna continued watching. Horace was right. The woman was late forties at a guess, wearing designer gear with a figure to die for, apart from being a little top-heavy. She had long, flowing highlighted fair hair.

"For once, I agree with you. She's in her prime. How old do you suppose she is? Fifty's the new forty, you know."

"She's forty-nine," said Elsa. "Mary Anne Beider from Germany. Twice divorced with no kids and she's a vegetarian." Elsa gave a look of disapproval whilst revealing the last detail.

Edna's eyes widened. "You're full of surprises tonight, Elsa. How on earth did you find all that out in such a short space of time?"

"I showed her up to her room. She's nice, very chatty and down to earth… excuse me, it looks like I'm needed." Elsa left with her tray and moments later was serving champagne to a red-headed man and his black-haired wife.

"I don't think Marge was expecting any of them to bring spouses, although she hid her surprise at the extra guest well," said Edna, watching the man gobbling down his drink almost as soon as he got it and taking another before Elsa could move away.

"If that's his wife, I'm a chameleon," said Horace.

"What makes you say if? I'm sure they introduced themselves as Mr and Mrs McCleary."

"Call it a chap's intuition. It's the way he looks at her. Even the best marriages don't keep the fires burning that hot… unless, of course, he's divorced and recently remarried."

"What are their first names again? I'm hopeless at names these days and the introductions were so hurried with the blasted Marcus shoving in every two minutes."

"Colm and Melissa. I understand he's from Dublin, but that's all I know. And you're right about Singleton butting in. I can't take to that fellow at all."

Edna looked at the smarmy Colm McCleary with his bulging beer belly. She guessed he was around forty, with a shock of red hair and a concave face. He looked like one of those men who was born in a suit and has never done a hard day's work in his life.

"His grin reminds me of a fox," she remarked.

"She's another looker, though," said Horace with a cheeky smile.

"Oh, don't start with your flirting again, Horace Tyler. You're too old for any of these women, as well you know."

Horace's hand went to his chest. "Daggers to my heart again, Edna Parkinton. A man likes to dream."

Edna laughed, happy to be with her friends again. It could be so lonely at home without her Dennis, but being with Horace, Fred and Marge was like… well, home. Her eyes turned to the large reception room where they were having pre-dinner drinks. With its decor hardly changed over the years, it reminded her of a bygone age. What parties Marge and Ralph must have had in this house. A life like this could have been hers if it wasn't for her father being disinherited.

"What are you thinking?" Horace's words dragged her from her reverie.

"Nothing much. You know, I don't feel as angry about missing out on all of this as I used to. I hate to admit it, but my dad got what he deserved."

Horace put a protective arm around her shoulder. "Bravo. Now, let's rescue Fred from Mr Melville and Mr Cartwright."

"Who are Mr Melville and Mr Cartwright?"

"You really don't remember names, do you? We met them when they arrived, along with Christina Makepeace who I don't think you took to."

"What makes you say that?" Horace was right. Edna hadn't liked the way Christina had waltzed in as if she owned the place, as well as trying to ingratiate herself with Marge the whole time.

"It was the look in your eye," said Horace. "Anyway, Melville's the young guy who looks more like a bodyguard than a businessman and Cartwright is the tubby Welshman. Fred's not comfortable in this sort of company."

Horace steered Edna around the room, closing in on Fred, who was looking like a deer caught in headlights. Edna couldn't understand the slight man's inhibitions. He had been a capable pharmacist for all his career and married to a doctor, but he wasn't good with wealth.

"I don't think our Fred is at ease in any company. I don't know what Marge sees in him."

"Now, now, Edna. Play nicely," said Horace.

"Hello," Fred looked and sounded relieved. "Have you met Bruce and Elmur? These are my friends Edna and Horace," he said.

Edna felt a pang of guilt when he referred to her as a friend. She liked him really, but couldn't help herself when it came to belittling people. She really must make more of an effort.

"We were introduced briefly," she said.

"Tell me about your businesses," said Horace. Unlike Fred, Horace was at ease in any company, but then he'd run a successful international aeronautics business and met with people across the world. Not only that, despite being self-absorbed, he could talk business all day long and seemed to know a little about everything.

Edna glazed over while the men discussed deals, productivity, price increases and management. She tuned back in when they moved onto the personal. Elmur Cartwright, who was overweight with dark blue eyes, wavy brown hair and a lilting Welsh accent, told them he was from Swansea.

"I didn't realise we could bring our wives," he said, "or I'd have brought my Glenis."

"Do you have children?" Horace asked.

"The younger one has just left to go to university in Cardiff and the older is in her final year at Cambridge." Elmur preened.

"She must be bright," said Edna, noticing Marge joining them and standing next to Fred.

"Yes, she's studying cellular biology. We're proud of her."

"Bruce here is from Paris," said Fred, attempting to draw the younger man back into the conversation.

Edna looked up at Bruce Melville, whose eyes were fixed on the attractive Elsa. *A womaniser,* she thought.

"Paris is such a beautiful city," said Marjorie, speaking for the first time. "I'm sorry to interrupt, but we will serve dinner in ten minutes. Please make your way through into the dining room when you're ready."

Bruce made a hasty retreat after spotting Marcus Singleton heading in their direction. He needn't have bothered. Singleton had his eyes on Elmur, who frowned when the officious man drew him towards the dining room.

"Have you met everyone?" Marge asked Edna.

"Not quite, but I think I know who they all are now." Edna drew Marge to one side. "That man, Marcus, is a pain in the rear, Marge. Why is he so obnoxious? He's already had an argument with Mary Anne Beider; he's ruining the atmosphere."

"I haven't taken to him either, Edna, but I have no say in the matter. He works for Jeremy. I suppose he must know what he's doing. It's not the way Ralph conducted business, but perhaps this cutthroat approach is the modern way." Marge's eyes betrayed her worry as they watched Marcus snarling while hissing something in Elmur's ear.

"Maybe you're right about that. If he gets out of hand, I'll ask Horace to take him to one side and give the man one of his pep talks, because your Jeremy seems oblivious." Edna noticed Marge flinching and regretted mentioning her son. "Horace can be tactful when he wants to be."

"I can't thank you all enough for coming," said Marge. "It's so good to have friends one can rely on. Do you think Frederick is all right, though? He seems uncomfortable."

Edna was about to say something scathing, but instead said, "He's fine. He was getting on well with Bruce Melville and Elmur Cartwright earlier, so don't worry about him."

"That's good to hear. I haven't really spoken to Bruce yet, apart from a brief welcome. Marcus interrupted before we had the opportunity to chat." Marge sighed heavily.

"He's built more like an all-in wrestler than a businessman," Edna said, laughing. They were standing at the edge of the dining room, waiting for people to choose their seats. Fred and Horace were hanging back too, while Jeremy gave directions. "Changing the subject, I hear we're going to a Christmas market tomorrow."

"Oh, I wasn't thinking of going myself. Do you think we should?"

"Absolutely," said Edna, taking Marge's arm. "You know how much I love shopping."

"I wouldn't want to intrude."

"Faith already suggested we go as well," said Fred, joining them, "and I could do with picking up a few last-minute presents."

"In that case, how can I refuse?" Marge said. "But first, let's get dinner over with and make sure Marcus doesn't upset anyone else."

Edna wondered whether Marge was referring to her housekeeper or Mary Anne Beider, but it was too late to ask as one of the waiting staff interrupted Marge.

Chapter 7

It wasn't too far to walk to Hampstead Heath Christmas market, but most of the guests wanted to take taxis, so Faith had arranged for two to transport them. Marjorie conceded she wouldn't have been able to manage the walk herself. Jeremy had flatly refused to cancel his plans, most likely at the bidding of Octavia, so Marjorie would have to put up with Marcus Singleton for the day and try to keep him under control.

Faith would do the bulk of the organising, and once they were at the market, the guests could all wander around independently. She had informed Marjorie it was a German-style market with entertainment, rides, stalls and such like. Frederick was hopping up and down like an excited child, which made Marjorie smile.

She had gone in search of Gina first thing, feeling terribly guilty about not having phoned the night before. Her housekeeper had appeared to be back to her normal self, although there was no time to talk with Sally preparing breakfasts and people sending down for drinks and extras as if they were staying in a hotel.

When Marjorie returned to the kitchen later to check the packed lunches were ready, Hercules had inched his way from the scullery to an invisible line between the kitchen and the hallway where he stood, rooted to the spot.

"Someone looks unhappy," Marjorie said.

"Don't mind him," replied Sally. "He's sulking because I slept in and didn't get the chance to take him out for a run. He's not had his breakfast either, what with the guests wanting so many different things."

"I'm sorry about that. I didn't expect it."

"I don't know how you could have," said Gina, smiling. "We've had the McClearys wanting breakfast in bed, Bruce Melville demanding a vegetable smoothie using his own recipe…" she waved a piece of paper in the air, "…Ms Beider who only drinks soya milk…"

I wonder what she had in her tea last night, Marjorie thought.

"…which we had to send out for, and Elmur Cartwright expecting a full English breakfast. The only ones who have been no trouble are your friends."

Sally cleared her throat.

"Don't tell me. Edna was starving and needed extra toast," Marjorie sighed.

Sally laughed. "I like her; she makes me howl. But don't worry, we've compiled a list of likes and dislikes now, so unless any of them decide to go fruitarian, tomorrow's breakfast will run like clockwork."

Marjorie put a hand to her mouth. "What about lunches?"

"It appears they're not as fussy about lunch as they are about breakfast. I've prepared a selection of sandwiches: egg and cress, salmon and soft cheese, and ham and pickle. There's also a piece of fruit each and clearly labelled flasks containing all their favourite drinks, including a little container of soya milk."

"Thank you so much. Is Mary Anne happy with egg and cress?"

Sally nodded. The waiting staff, or temps as Edna referred to them, appeared when they had finished talking.

"You can take them up. They're all clearly labelled." Sally didn't seem to be shy of giving out her own orders.

"There's a Mr Singleton upstairs asking for Lady Marjorie," replied one of the temporary staff.

Marjorie exhaled. "Oh dear. I don't think I added him to the list of lunches."

"Gina prepared his herself," said Sally with a mischievous twinkle in her eye.

Marjorie didn't have time to question that because she could hear her name being called from the main hall. "I'd better go. Try to get some rest today, Gina. The others will do the guest rooms under Elsa's supervision."

On arrival in the hallway, she discovered the reason for her being summoned was because Marcus Singleton couldn't find his coat. Why he thought Marjorie would have anything to do with it going missing, she did not know.

"Have you tried the study?" she suggested.

Moments later, he returned with the same heavy overcoat he had been wearing when he tested her doorbell to its limits. "I didn't put it in there," he complained, mumbling away to anyone who would listen. And no-one was.

Marjorie hurried to the front door, where things felt chaotic with people behaving as if they were going to miss out on the outing. Both taxis had arrived. Once everyone had collected their own personal goody bag from the hall table, Faith, who had arrived early, corralled them into the cars.

"Mr and Mrs McCleary, you're in the first car with Ms Beider and Mrs Makepeace. Elmur, you, Bruce and Mr Singleton are with me in the second."

"I need to speak to Colm McCleary and Mrs Makepeace, she…" Marcus pointed to Mary Anne Beider, "can travel in the car behind."

Colm McCleary rolled his eyes and whispered something in his wife's ear; she giggled. Mary Anne Beider didn't budge at first, but then followed Faith slowly to the other taxi, looking put out.

"Why don't you travel with Marjorie and the others?" Horace suggested to Mary Anne. "I'll squash up with the others."

"Thank you," Marjorie mouthed to him as he joined Elmur and Bruce in the back of the second taxi, Faith climbing into the front seat.

"How are we going to get there with only two taxis?" Mary Anne asked, but grinned when she saw Johnson drawing up in the Rolls. "Ah, this will do nicely," she said.

The journey was relatively short, but Marjorie managed to find out that Mary Anne was twice divorced and had kept her second husband's surname.

"He's quite famous in Germany, so it made sense to use his name like he used me."

"Do you have any children?" Edna asked. This was a topic Marjorie usually steered clear of because it could open a whole host of complications and sensitivities, but Mary Anne didn't seem to mind.

"I never wanted kids. It's hard enough for a woman to do business without taking years out to have a family. Besides, if you had met either of my husbands, you wouldn't want to bring their offspring into the world."

Marjorie nudged Edna before she could ask something plain like why Mary Anne married them then. Although the question was on Marjorie's mind too.

"What is it you do?" Frederick asked.

"My company makes small electronic devices that sell for thousands of euros each. We're hoping to do business with Lady Marjorie's son, although I would be open to sharing the contract with any of the others."

"That explains why you're all so pally with each other," said Edna. "Horace and I noticed that last night."

More like Horace noticed, thought Marjorie, who knew Edna's observational skills usually centred around herself. *Don't be unkind, Snellthorpe,* she told herself.

"You don't have to trample your competitors to get the best deals. You never know when you might need them, and sometimes you might want to buy them out a few years down the road."

"Do you think you'll get the contract?" Edna asked before Marjorie could nudge her again.

"Not if Marcus Singleton has anything to do with it, but I'm hoping Jeremy will be more pragmatic."

The car pulled up just when Marjorie would have liked to ask what Mary Anne meant by that last sentence.

Once they were walking through the busy market, most of the guests followed Faith, who gave them directions and told them when and where they could meet to get a taxi back.

"If any of you wants me to stay with you, just let me know," she said.

With no takers, Faith turned to Marjorie. "Would you like me to stick around?"

"Not unless you want to. We've taken up enough of your time."

"In that case, I'll go home to Mum. She took one of her funny turns this morning."

"Oh dear, I'm sorry," said Marjorie.

"I expect it had more to do with me leaving her, but don't worry. I'll be able to take them to Madame Tussauds and Harrods tomorrow as planned."

Marjorie would be eternally grateful to Faith for stepping in like this. She watched her walk away before turning into the crowded market. Horace had joined Edna, and they were already eyeing up the hat stalls. There was no likelihood of losing Edna, who today was wearing her bright red wig. It almost matched Colm McCleary's hair, except his was natural.

"Shall we walk?"

Frederick offered Marjorie his arm, and she took it rather than retrieve her fold-up walking stick from her handbag.

"Do you think Marcus and Mary Anne know each other?" she asked as they started through the crowds milling around.

"It sounded like it. Either that or he's sexist as well as rude."

"But he said he wanted to speak to Christina Makepeace and Colm McCleary."

Frederick made a spluttering sound. She turned to check he was all right, but he was chuckling.

"She's not his wife."

"Oh. Who is she then?"

"His mistress. I wanted to know more about them all, so I checked them out online and on social media. The real Mrs McCleary, who has lovely green eyes and blonde hair, is on a skiing holiday with their three children."

Annoyed at being taken for a fool by the fake married couple, Marjorie pursed her lips.

"I see. What did you find out about the others?"

"Not a lot. Most of them are boring businesspeople like I once was. They have LinkedIn accounts, but they're all to do with business. The only one using the other social media platforms is Bruce, but it's all about health and muscle workouts. He's quite the fanatic in his spare time."

"Is he married?"

"Not from what I could see, but there are lots of photos of him and a beautiful young woman who lives in Budapest. I assume she's his girlfriend."

"Was there anything on Marcus Singleton?"

Frederick cleared his throat. "Not exactly. Oh, hang on. I want to look at this stall; there might be something for the grandkids."

Marjorie was thankful she had worn a thick coat and hat. It had turned out to be a bright but ice-cold day with remnants of frost on the stall roofs. The market was alive with shoppers, most of them family groups with children and a few dogs. She grinned inwardly, imagining Hercules strolling through the market and everyone giving him a wide berth. The vendors were selling all kinds of Christmassy things, from food and toys to angel decorations. The stalls themselves were decorated with a bright array of reds and greens, with tinsel spread around the sides and front.

As they meandered along, Marjorie found herself getting lost in the atmosphere and enjoying the Christmas songs. A band played Christmas carols from a central point further on, where a choir was singing and collecting for the homeless. Marjorie took a note from her purse and dropped it into one of the buckets while she and Frederick paused to listen for a few minutes. Aromas from the meat stalls made her mouth water and the leafy scent of cinnamon and nutmeg blended with the crisp wintry air.

"Shall we have lunch? There are some tables over there," said Frederick.

"Is that the time already? I haven't had this much fun at Christmas since—"

Frederick squeezed her arm. "Me neither," he breathed.

Marjorie felt her eyes sting, suddenly recalling the times she and her late husband had wandered through the Christmas markets in Germany and Amsterdam. She blinked away a tear threatening to fall while they walked towards a large square where tables had been set up and a gigantic Christmas tree took centre stage. Halogen heaters stood all around the square, which was next door to a false ice rink full of adults and children skating.

Frederick paused at a food stall and bought them mince pies. "It wouldn't be the same without a treat," he explained.

Marjorie decided to ask Sally to bake some mince pies and check there would be some Christmas treats served over the next few days. She noticed a few of her guests pausing at stalls, smiling and laughing together. They seemed to be having fun. But as she was not looking where she was going, she crashed into someone who rounded on her.

"Why the hell don't you watch where you're going?" Marcus Singleton yelled at her, his eyes bulging.

Frederick stepped between them. "There's no need to shout," he said, looking up at the taller man.

Marcus calmed a little. "I didn't realise it was you." He looked at Marjorie, but didn't apologise. Instead, he took a large bite of his sandwich and swished it down with whatever was in his flask.

Suddenly, Marcus turned bright red, struggling for breath as he clutched at his neck with both hands before falling to the ground. There was a commotion as some people gathered around the man thrashing and writhing on the ground, while others walked by, oblivious.

Marjorie heard someone phoning for an ambulance while Frederick bent down over Marcus. The man was now still as Frederick placed trembling fingers on his neck. His grey eyes met Marjorie's with a look of disbelief. He shook his head.

"I'm a doctor. Give him some room," Marjorie heard a woman call out. Everyone stepped aside while the young doctor and someone identifying themselves as a nurse examined Marcus and began pounding on his chest.

It was obvious Marcus was dead before the paramedics arrived and took over.

Frederick pulled Marjorie away from the commotion to the food square. "Come on, let's get a hot drink inside you. You're ever so pale."

Minutes later, she and Frederick were huddled around a heater, drinking tea and staring at their sandwiches.

"At least it was quick," said Frederick. "I'd like to go like that."

Marjorie's thoughts were elsewhere. "What if…" she paused.

"What is it, Marjorie?" Frederick's eyes oozed compassion.

"Gina prepared his lunch. The one he was eating when he collapsed. He upset her, you see."

Horace and Edna joined them before Frederick had any time to respond. Edna wheezed when she sat down.

"You'll never guess what, Marge. Marcus Singleton had a heart attack."

"I was there and I don't believe it was a heart attack," Marjorie responded. "I'm sure the man was poisoned."

"Goodness me," said Horace. "Not again."

Edna opened her mouth as if to argue, but stopped herself. Frederick shook his head, speaking softly.

"He was eating his lunch at the time."

Edna had been about to take a bite of her sandwich, but dropped it again.

"I don't think you need to worry," said Marjorie. "All the lunches were labelled."

"In that case," said Edna, ramming the sandwich into her mouth.

A lump of lead settled in Marjorie's stomach and an ice-cold chill ran through her.

Chapter 8

Marjorie's chauffeur took her and Edna home, leaving Frederick and Horace to track down the rest of the guests and break the news of the unfortunate demise of Marcus Singleton. Edna was being generally empathetic with Marjorie's train of thought. After initially suggesting the cook might be responsible for poisoning Marcus, if indeed that's what it turned out to be, she changed tack when Marjorie told her that Mrs Ratton had prepared his lunch.

Before Marjorie had even taken off her hat and coat, Edna burst out with what they were both thinking.

"So, you believe your housekeeper poisoned the guy, Marge. But why would she?"

"I don't know. It all started with the tea tray."

"You're going to have to explain that comment." Edna took Marjorie's outdoor clothing from her and hung it up with her own hat and coat before leading her towards the sitting room. Elsa happened to be descending the stairs at the same time.

"I thought I heard the door. You're back early. Did you have a good time?" she asked.

"It was eventful," said Edna.

"Do you think we could have a pot of tea?" Marjorie asked.

"I'll do it now. Sally's gone upstairs for a rest and Gina nipped out to the shops to buy more soya milk, cheese and suchlike. We thought you would be out all day."

Marjorie felt herself stiffen at the mention of her housekeeper. "We'll be in the small sitting room."

"Are you all right, Lady… I mean Marjorie? You are ever so pale."

"She'll be fine once she's had a hot cup of tea," said Edna. "It's freezing out there. We'd have been better off staying here in the warm."

"Is it just tea for two?"

"Yeah. The men are still at the market, and they say it's women who like to shop," Edna said, laughing.

"Right then. I won't be long."

Marjorie could see from her expression that Elsa's sharp mind knew something was amiss, but her housemaid held her tongue and scurried off towards the kitchen.

"Don't overplay your hand; we're going to have to tell her what happened soon enough," Marjorie said once they were in the sitting room. The painting of Ralph's parents looking down from the mantelpiece gave Marjorie a sense of calm again. The open fire radiated heat; Marjorie huddled close, feeling a sudden chill.

She looked at Edna, who seemed hurt. "But thank you for your understanding. I would rather no-one know about Marcus's death until I've spoken to Gina."

"I take it Gina's Mrs Ratton's first name?"

"Yes. She sometimes prefers Mrs Ratton when working, but under the circumstances, she may need a friend."

"You still haven't answered my question. What was it about the tea tray?"

Marjorie undid the top button of her cardigan, which helped her to breathe. She explained how Gina had come out of the kitchen when she had taken Marcus and Jeremy to meet the staff and dropped the tray, sending bone china flying across the floor.

"I was shocked, because she's not usually clumsy, but initially I put it down to the stress," Marjorie said. "But then Mrs Ratton… Gina started to act in ways that were so out of character before leaving early to go home, suffering from a headache, without telling me. I also suspected something was amiss when, after you arrived, Elsa told us that Marcus had gone to the kitchen."

"Which is why you rushed off like a bat out of hell?" Edna quizzed.

"I wouldn't quite put it like that, but yes. I wanted to make sure Marcus would not upset her any further. He was such an overbearing man, wasn't he? Anyway, I was too late; he told me he'd already had words with her. You can imagine how furious I felt at his impertinence."

"Was that before or after the incident with the dog?"

"Before. He had already done his worst when I found Hercules growling at him."

"Elsa told me and Horace last night that Marcus had upset your housekeeper somehow, but she didn't know what had happened because she heard about it second hand. Sally told her. Don't you think you should call Jeremy and let him know what's happened to his negotiator? Not that he would have got anywhere with most of your guests avoiding the man."

Marjorie shook her head vigorously. "Not until I've spoken to Gina. She won't be long at the shops."

There was a knock at the sitting-room door. Elsa brought in a tea trolley with a pot of tea and slices of cake.

"I thought you might need some sugar, you looking pale and all." Elsa poured their tea before asking, "Would you like anything else before I have me lunch?"

"Haven't you eaten yet?" Edna asked.

"No. I wanted to make sure them outsiders did the rooms properly before they left. They haven't long gone."

"Thank you, Elsa. You enjoy your lunch," Marjorie said.

Once Elsa had left, Edna hissed, "How will we know when Gina's back?"

"We'll enjoy our tea, and then I'll return the trolley. She'll be emptying the tumble dryer or ironing. We often chat while she does the ironing in the afternoons. I expect she'll want to be certain the tablecloths are lily white before setting the table for tonight's dinner. What I'm worried about is how I'm going to ask a woman who has worked under my roof for thirty years, and is someone I consider a friend, whether she poisoned one of the guests."

"Are you sure it wasn't a heart attack? I can't think where your Gina would even get hold of poison, let alone know how to use it. I'm sure I wouldn't know where to find any."

Edna had a point. Marjorie couldn't say for certain why she felt someone had poisoned the man, but there was something amiss.

"I know what it was," she said as if Edna had been privy to her inner ramblings. "He didn't clutch his chest, and he looked as if he was choking when he collapsed. Then there were the convulsions."

"Maybe he had some food stuck. I've heard people can die like that. You have to punch them in the stomach or something."

"Heaven help me if I ever choke with you around. You're talking about the abdominal thrust manoeuvre, but it wasn't that sort of choking. Anyway, back to the poison scenario: if we have any poison at all, it will be rat poison kept in the shed. Although I asked the gardener not to use it after discovering it makes the poor creatures bleed internally, so we might not even have any. Either way, that's not what was used today.

"You might be right, Edna, I wonder if I'm just jumping to conclusions because of our history. As you say, Marcus Singleton could have died from a heart attack or even a stroke. His blood pressure must have been through the roof. Men with temperaments like his usually have high blood pressure, don't they?"

"You've just said it wasn't a heart attack because he didn't clutch at his chest. Make your mind up."

"Now I think of it, I don't think every person who has a heart attack has chest pain, and as I said, it could have been a stroke. People have difficulty swallowing when they have a stroke, which would explain the choking."

"You mean the choking that wasn't choking," Edna slurped her tea before challenging Marjorie with her eyes. "So now you're saying he wasn't poisoned."

"I suppose I am. It must have been the shock of seeing a man die right in front of my eyes that made me think otherwise."

"And we have a track record of stumbling into murder, which might have coloured your judgement."

Marjorie tried hard to convince herself this wasn't one of those occasions. "As I said, he may have had high blood pressure."

"You're not fooling me, Marge. You're running scared."

"So what if I am? I've known Gina for decades and she is incapable of killing anyone. If I ask her, I might ruin years of trust."

"And if you don't and it turns out to be murder, it won't take the plods long to find out where the poison came from and who prepared his lunch. It would be kinder coming from you than from them."

Marjorie finished her tea and helped herself to another one. "Why don't you phone Horace and see if he's gathered any information from the market?"

"Good idea." Edna pulled out her mobile and dialled. Horace answered straight away. "Hiya, Horace. What's happening…? Right… Yep… Are you sure? Yeah, yeah, I'll tell Marge. What about the others? Seriously? I see. Okay. See you later."

"How on earth could he hear his telephone in that market with all the racket going on?" Marjorie asked.

"Never mind that. You won't believe it."

"He's tracked down the guests and they don't care and are continuing their shopping," said Marjorie.

"Not only that, but he also said they seemed almost joyful at hearing Marcus Singleton was out of the way. If it is murder, your housekeeper might not be the only suspect."

"Was there any news on that front?"

"Horace says the police are on scene and they've cordoned off the area where Marcus collapsed. A doctor who attended him insisted they were called."

"I see," said Marjorie. Her heart raced a little faster. "That must have been the doctor Frederick and I saw trying to resuscitate him. I think it's time to speak to Gina." Edna stood up, but Marjorie held a hand out. "I'd better do this alone. I wouldn't want her to think we're ganging up on her. I'll inform her of the man's death and see where that leads."

Edna's mouth drooped and her shoulders sagged. Marjorie didn't want to upset her, but couldn't trust her to be subtle in a situation like this.

"You could break the news to Elsa and ask if she noticed anything unusual this morning."

Edna's eyes lit up again. "Brilliant idea. She lunches in the library, doesn't she?"

"You're more observant than you make out, Edna Parkinton. Yes, that's where she'll be. You two appear to get on well, and Elsa likes a gossip, so try to get her talking without letting on the death is suspicious; you'll glean more information that way."

Edna stroked her chin. "You can rely on me."

Marjorie hoped she had done the right thing when she watched Edna rush happily from the room. But it was better than the alternative, which would be Edna moping around feeling she was being left out. Marjorie took a deep breath before returning all the cups to the trolley. Neither of them had touched the cake.

The crockery wobbled dangerously at the beginning of her journey because her hands were shaking so much. Her strength wasn't what it used to be.

You can do this, Marjorie told herself as she pushed the trolley along the hallway, walking purposefully towards the kitchen.

Chapter 9

Edna strolled into Marjorie's library with its extensive book collection. The familiar smell of polish mingling with leather and paper made her want to take a deep intake of breath. Bookshelves covered every wall. Sunlight from the large window made the polished shelves sparkle.

Edna enjoyed a good historical novel herself, but the books in this room impressed her. Bindings of reds, blues, blacks, and greens brought the room alive. These books were well read, mostly by her late cousin, Ralph Snellthorpe, but Marjorie also enjoyed reading and said she reread some classics over and over. Rereading books was something Edna couldn't get her head around; with so many new books to try, why read the same ones? She shook her head at the thought.

The library was quiet. Elsa hadn't heard her come in and was sitting in a brown leather chair with her feet on a matching stool, engrossed in a novel.

Edna took a few steps forward, hearing her heels clop across the hardwood floor. Elsa pulled her feet from the stool and sat up.

"I didn't hear anyone come in. Do you need something?"

"Sorry to disturb your break," said Edna. "Marge thought you should know there was an incident this morning. That's why she was out of sorts."

"I knew there was something. What sort of incident?"

"I'm afraid Marcus Singleton has died."

Opening and closing her mouth like a goldfish, Elsa spoke eventually. "How? Where? Was he run over?"

"No, nothing like that. It looked like a heart attack. Marge and Fred were there when he collapsed."

"Poor Marjorie. As if she ain't got enough on her plate. That's all she needs this week. I can't say I'm surprised, mind, the way he tore through his steak last night and the amount of cream he poured on his pudding clogging up his arteries. What with that and his temper, he was a heart attack waiting to happen. He reminded me of a grouchy uncle I had when I was little. He dropped dead at his desk – probably while counting out his money."

Edna suppressed a grin. Normally she would enjoy a conversation like this, but she was on a mission.

"How did he seem to you this morning?" she asked.

"I didn't see much of him, to be honest. I just let him in while everyone was having breakfast. Mrs Ratton refused to answer the door in case it was him. She really didn't take to him, you know. Anyway, he waltzed straight into Marjorie's study as if he owned the place and had a meeting with Elmur. He's a nice bloke, he is."

"I thought you said we were eating breakfast."

"Yeah, but I had to haul Elmur away from his second fry up. He wasn't too happy about it, I can tell you."

"Did he say so?"

"No. It was the way he rolled his eyes, huffing and puffing and moaning about not being given any peace."

"Do you know what their meeting was about?"

"I guess it was to do with who gets the contract with Jeremy's business, but they weren't on friendly terms. I heard Elmur telling Marcus he wasn't going to stand for it."

"Stand for what?" Edna asked.

"I'm not sure, but I expect it was his bullish behaviour he meant, and being called away from his breakfast and all. I asked if they needed anything. Marcus demanded tea and told me to close the door. I felt like pouring tea all over him when I took it back."

Edna had to suppress another grin. "And you heard nothing else they said?"

"Nope. When I took the tea in, the door was open again, and Elmur had already left. Marcus was humming a tune, looking smug like, so maybe the negotiations went well. I didn't see him again except for when he was in the hallway looking at Marjorie's paintings. Him and Christina were having a conversation about art. I guess she was being polite, because I didn't get the impression she knew much about it."

Edna was tempted to ask how Elsa worked that out, but as she herself was ignorant on the subject, she didn't want to embarrass herself.

"Did you see him get his lunch?"

"No, the outsiders sorted that out. I suppose they'll all be leaving now, won't they?"

Edna didn't know which group Elsa was referring to, but she didn't think the houseguests or the temps would be going anywhere.

"I'm not sure. At the moment, the guests are carrying on with their shopping. From what Horace told me, they weren't that concerned."

"They'll all be at Mr Jeremy like vultures now, then? It will work out for the best. Gina will be pleased, anyway." Elsa's hand flew to her mouth. "Not pleased he's dead, mind, just pleased he won't be around. It'll be nice to see her back to her normal self again."

"Did you see anyone else with Marcus after Elmur and Christina?"

Elsa closed her book. "No. I was trying to keep an eye on them outside helps. They kept mixing things up. I'd better break the news to Gina… Mrs Ratton."

"There's no need to do that. Marge's doing it as we speak."

"What's going on?" Elsa's eyes burned into Edna's. This woman was nobody's fool.

"Why should anything be going on?"

"Marjorie breaking the news as if Gina might be upset like. He wasn't a relative or nothing; well, not one I knew about, anyway."

"I expect she wanted to let her know he wouldn't be getting under her feet anymore. If Gina knew him of old, it was clear the memory wasn't a happy one. Marge doesn't like it when any of you are upset."

Elsa thought for a moment before nodding. "She's good that way."

Edna was saved from having to reply by the doorbell.

"I'll get that, then I'll go upstairs and tell Sally what's happened." Elsa started walking towards the door before turning. "Unless Marjorie's breaking the news to her as well."

"Not that I know of. Why don't you go on up and tell her? I'll let whoever that is in. It might be Horace."

"If you're sure you don't mind."

Edna strolled towards the front door. "You forget, there are no housemaids where I live. I'm quite capable of opening a front door."

Elsa had already disappeared, which was perhaps as well. Edna didn't want to come across as bitter even though she felt resentment rising in her again. She swallowed it back before opening the door.

Horace was on the top step with Mary Anne Beider and Christina Makepeace. He grinned like the show off he was when trying to impress the ladies.

"Hello. The temperature is dropping outside, and the ladies had exhausted their desire for shopping, so I escorted them home. We walked."

That explained the ruddy cheeks. At least he hadn't been plying them with drinks. Mary Anne hopped up and down as if to show how cold it was.

"Do you mind?"

"No, of course not."

"You're blocking the entrance, Edna," Horace whispered.

"What? Oh, sorry." Edna stood aside and let the three of them into the hall. The women removed their coats, holding them out to her. Edna kept her arms by her side and Horace just caught Mary Anne's coat before it fell to the floor. He then took Christina's.

"Why don't you ladies go through to the small sitting room? I'll see if I can get us a hot toddy," he said.

"Ooh, that sounds perfect. Come on, Mary Anne."

Mary Anne followed Christina, but not before shooting Edna a wary look.

"What was that all about?" asked Horace, hanging up the coats before removing his own and placing it on a hook.

"Who do they think they are? I'm not their servant."

"They were treating you like a host, not a servant. Honestly, Edna, you can be so prickly at times. They know we're friends of the household. You should take it as a compliment."

Edna didn't mind being challenged by most people – she could hold her own – but when it came to Horace, it was different. She hated disappointing him. As a rule, they got on so well and saw things in the same way.

"It must be the shock of seeing a dead body. Especially with Marge thinking we've got another murder on our hands. Did the police tell you anything?"

Horace put an arm around her, leading her to the sitting room. "Nothing more than I said over the phone. It's not looking good for the cook, though. They took the sandwich bag and scraped the lunch into forensic bags. A forensic team arrived just as we were leaving. Fred decided to hang about just in case."

"It wasn't the cook who prepared his lunch, it was Marge's housekeeper."

Horace's forehead creased. "The one he upset?"

"Exactly. Marge is with her now, breaking the news and asking some questions."

"Oh dear. Although I really can't imagine anyone in Marjorie's employ being responsible for Marcus's death. Things will turn out for the best. The troublesome man most likely had a heart attack and the doctor's being over diligent, calling the police in."

"Marge said it could have been a stroke. Did those two say anything about it?" Edna nodded towards the sitting-room door.

"Other than good riddance, no. I don't think they realise his death might be suspicious."

"So, they thought the forensics were out for an afternoon jolly, did they?"

Horace scratched his head. "Sarcasm doesn't become you, but you make a good point. Perhaps they know more than they're letting on."

"And you were too busy flirting to find out."

"I suppose I was. You know I can't help myself. Look, you go in there and pump them for information while I find this cook. At least we can be assured the tea won't be poisoned." Horace snorted a forced laugh, less convincing than his usual one.

"The cook's not there. Elsa's gone to fetch her. See if you can find out where Marge's got to. She went ages ago. And watch out for the dog." Edna giggled.

"Oh blimey! I forgot there was a gigantic beast called Hercules along that way."

Edna moved her head frantically, trying to warn him before he turned and almost fell over the mutt. Marjorie hadn't been kidding about the size of him. Sally, the said cook, appeared, as casually dressed as she had been the day before. Her black hair was tied back, and she appeared to be wearing the same jeans from the night before. She caught up with the dog.

"Sorry, he's in a rush. He gets hangry without food."

Horace took a step back. "As long as he doesn't eat human, he'll be fine. What's hangry anyway?"

Sally chuckled. "It's a word mashup of angry and hungry." She laughed again when Hercules wagged his long black tail and snuggled up to Horace's legs. Horace put a cautious hand out and patted him on the head.

"Obviously not an alpha male." Marjorie approached from the opposite direction, winking at Sally, who burst out laughing.

"Are you going to share the joke?" Edna hated being left out.

"Sally told me yesterday Hercules doesn't take to alpha males."

"I'm not sure how to take that," Horace feigned offence.

Edna snorted, patting him on the arm. "Your secret's safe with us."

Their laughter eased any tension Edna had been feeling.

"Would you like some tea?" Sally asked.

"I was rather hoping for something stronger. I know it's early, but would you have any hot toddies?" Horace asked.

"Leave the drinks that are up here for later. There's whisky in a cabinet in the kitchen. Elsa will show you where," said Marjorie.

"Hot toddies for three coming right up," Sally said.

"Five. Mary Anne and Christina are in the lounge," Horace said.

"I'm on it," said Sally.

"I would have preferred brandy," said Marjorie when the woman and dog left.

"It'll do you good," said Horace, reassuringly. "Very nice on the palate too. I fear we'll need our wits about us this evening." He lowered his voice. "What did your housekeeper say?"

"Not much. I'm afraid when I told her the man who had clearly had such a profound effect on her was no longer with us, she was so relieved, I couldn't bring myself to ask anything else. We had tea."

"I don't believe you, Marge! You're supping tea with a murderer while we're treading on eggshells here."

"You treading on eggshells I have to see. Stomping on them, more like," said Marjorie, sticking her chin out. "Besides, Gina is not a murderer. If Marcus was murdered, somebody else did it and we will find out who."

Marjorie strolled determinedly into the sitting room with Horace shooting Edna a warning glance not to say anything else. Exasperated, Edna followed them inside.

Chapter 10

The hot toddies were better than expected, and Horace had been quite right about how palatable and refreshing they were. Having helped themselves to drinks and seats, the company relaxed, helped by Horace's attentive manner. He played the charming host well, pouring and refilling their drinks from the antique whisky noggins Marjorie and Ralph had inherited from her late husband's parents. Sally or Elsa had made a good choice. Though rarely used, the noggins were ideal for serving hot toddies.

After two drinks, Christina Makepeace excused herself. "It's time I went upstairs to change for dinner."

"There will be pre-dinner drinks in the reception room from seven-thirty," said Marjorie.

"Wonderful. I'll see you all soon, then."

Mary Anne Beider didn't seem in any hurry to leave and was more at ease than she had been the previous evening. Marjorie remembered Edna telling her she and Horace had thought Mary Anne might have been arguing with Marcus.

"I'm sorry about your loss, Marjorie." Mary Anne was the first to mention what was foremost on everyone's mind.

"If you're referring to Mr Singleton, I didn't know him well. We only met for the first time yesterday, but it is a shock when someone dies so suddenly and right in front of you. Did you know him?"

A slight twitch of the rouged right cheek suggested Marjorie had hit a nerve. "Not really."

"What were you fighting about last night, then?" Edna's challenge came in her usual straight-for-the-jugular manner.

"I don't know what you mean." Mary Anne held her glass out for a refill and Horace obliged.

"Before dinner. Horace and I noticed you seemed to have a heated discussion. Not that anyone would blame you; dead or not, he seemed a dislikeable man."

Mary Anne relaxed. "Oh, that… we were discussing business. Marcus was keen to knock all the suppliers down to rock-bottom prices. We're used to it and are happy to compete against each other, but not at any price. At the end of the day, none of us are enemies, but Marcus was doing his best to pit us against each other. He's always been like that."

"Oh? I thought you said you didn't know him." Marjorie was on to the slip of the tongue in an instant.

Mary Anne flushed. "I didn't. But when you're a niche supplier, you get to know a lot about people, even if you don't know them well. I heard he was difficult to work with and moved from company to company. Your son would have got the measure of him eventually, I'm sure. Still, it seems his lifestyle caught up with him in the end. He ate too much, drank too much and womanised too much."

"Is that something you know to be true or is it also hearsay?" asked Edna.

"It's what I heard. If you want to know more about Marcus Singleton, speak to Christina."

"Why?" Edna's eyes narrowed.

"Come, come, ladies," Horace intervened. "A man has died. We don't really need to pick him to pieces when he's barely cold, do we?"

"You're right," said Mary Anne, smiling at Horace before turning her attention back to Marjorie. "I hope Jeremy is going to be all right about us continuing our negotiations. We've all given up other plans to come here at short notice."

"Good heavens!" Marjorie jumped up. "I haven't even told Jeremy yet. Everything's been such a blow. I'll call him now."

Mary Anne took the cue and got up. "In that case, I'd better change for dinner. Please pass on my condolences, but if you could also let him know we are keen to continue with our business discussions, I'd be most grateful."

As soon as Mary Anne was out of the room, Edna rounded on Horace. "Well, thanks very much, Horace Tyler."

"Leave it, Edna. Horace was quite right to let her feel someone is on her side. She knows a lot more than she's letting on, and I think Horace's ploy will endear him to her. It won't be long before she confides in him."

"Was it a ploy?" Edna challenged.

Horace tapped his nose. "What do you think?" he said, eyes twinkling.

"Humph." Edna folded her arms.

"We also need to find out what it is Christina Makepeace knows," said Marjorie. "Did you get anywhere with Elsa, Edna?"

"Not really. The only person who spent any real time with Marcus this morning was Elmur. She had to deliver a summons."

"I saw that. I assumed it was a telephone call," said Horace.

"Well, I didn't notice anything," Edna snapped as though it were Horace's fault she had missed the interaction.

"You were, erm... tucking into your breakfast and chatting to Colm McCleary's, erm... wife."

Tucking into your breakfast was right, thought Marjorie, but said, "Melissa isn't Colm's wife."

"We could have told you that, Marge."

Horace shot Edna a look which implied he had been the one to make the discovery before saying, "We weren't certain, though. How did you find out?"

"From Frederick. He's researched all the guests, and it turns out Colm's wife, who looks nothing like the woman purporting to be Mrs McCleary, is on a skiing trip with their children. Where is Frederick, by the way?"

"I left him sniffing around the cordoned area," said Horace. "He was doing a terrible job of pretending to look at baubles when I told him I was bringing the ladies home. It was obvious he was trying to pick up anything the police had to say."

"A proper little detective your Fred's turning out to be, Marge."

"He's not *my* Fred, and his name's Frederick," Marjorie said through gritted teeth.

"Hey! Keep yer 'air on."

"I'm not the one wearing a wig," said Marjorie, but regretted saying it the minute it was out of her mouth. It wasn't Edna's fault she had post-chemotherapy alopecia.

Edna took it in good grace. "Okay, I get it. He's not your Fred… er… ick."

"I apologise for the wig reference," said Marjorie, appreciating Edna's effort.

"And a very nice one it is too," said Horace. "That red's my favourite colour."

Edna cradled her hair with both hands, patting it in place and smiling. "That's why I wore it today. I might go blonde tonight, though. Or should I wear the purple one?"

"Blonde," Horace and Marjorie spoke in unison. Any tension in the atmosphere had been broken, and they all laughed together.

"You really should phone Jeremy, Marge. He ought to know," Edna said.

"You're quite right." Marjorie walked to the corner of the room and picked up the telephone, dialling Jeremy's number. She watched Edna and Horace bantering and Elsa bring in another tray of drinks.

"I thought you might like some more," Marjorie heard her say.

"Hello, Mother. What can I do for you?" Jeremy's speech was slurred.

She was about to ask him how he knew it was her, but then remembered how mobile phones brought up the caller identity.

"I'm afraid I've got some bad news, Jeremy."

"What? Just a minute… I'll take this next door…"

Marjorie waited while he removed himself from a room where there was a lot of happy chattering.

"… I couldn't hear you very well. What bad news? Don't tell me Marcus has sent someone packing? I told him to tone it down."

"No, it's nothing like that. I'm sorry to tell you that Marcus Singleton is dead."

The phone went silent. She wondered if her son had taken in what she had just said.

"Dead? What do you mean, dead?"

"He collapsed while we were at the market around lunchtime. A doctor was nearby and attended to him, but they pronounced him dead at the scene. The police were called."

"Hang on a minute. He died at lunchtime? What time is it now?"

Marjorie looked at the grandfather clock in the corner of the room. "Six-thirty."

"Why didn't you call me when it happened?"

As if you would have come running, thought Marjorie, but said, "Never mind that now, Jeremy. The man's dead, but your guests, according to Mary Anne Beider, would like to continue negotiations."

"Good. At least that's something. We need this contract sorted."

"Will you be joining us for dinner this evening?"

There was a pause at the other end of the telephone while Jeremy processed what he had been told. "This is most inconvenient," he said.

"Marcus's death, or your coming for dinner?" Marjorie saw Edna's quizzical look out of the corner of her eye.

"Both, as a matter of fact. Cut the sarcasm, Mother. This is business too."

"It sounds more like a party, from what I can hear." The music and laughter had become louder wherever Jeremy was speaking from.

"I'll be there in a minute… Shut the door, will you?" her son snapped.

"It sounds as though you're busy, so I won't keep you. If it's not too much trouble, perhaps we'll see you for the tour tomorrow?"

"Gosh, is that still going ahead? I suppose none of them are that upset about Marcus. To be honest, it might be for the best. He was becoming more of a liability than an asset, especially since we've been talking to these potential new suppliers. He has, or rather had, history with some of them. Tried to freeze Mary Anne out of the talks altogether, but she contacted me direct. Her firm's high on my list to get the contract, but I'll have to speak to all of them before I decide. Maybe it's not such a bad thing after all."

"You haven't answered the question." Marjorie was growing impatient.

"We're staying here overnight and most of tomorrow. You keep them entertained and I'll start official talks tomorrow evening."

"Tomorrow evening?"

"I'm tied up all day tomorrow and can't get away until then. Marcus was going to kick things off. Look, I'm sorry, Mother, but it was you who organised the outings in the first place. I'd better go. But… wait… did you say the police were called? Routine, I suppose."

"Yes, I did say that. The doctor who tried to help Marcus felt the police should be informed, so if I were you, I wouldn't mention anything to them about your relief at losing your chief negotiator. They might misinterpret it."

"You can't be serious?"

"I don't joke about such things, Jeremy. You go back to your party while I entertain *your* guests. Perhaps I'll start the negotiations myself."

"Mother. Don't—" Jeremy was still protesting at the other end of the line when Marjorie returned the handset to its base.

"Good for you," said Edna, who must have been listening in.

"What did he say?" Horace asked.

"That Marcus's demise might not be a bad thing for business, and he'll be here tomorrow evening."

"I know that look, Marge," Edna said.

"What look?" said Marjorie, strolling across the room and helping herself to a second hot toddy.

Chapter 11

Frederick hung around where the police cordon had been set up, pretending to look at Christmas decorations on the busy stall next door to the one where Marcus had collapsed. He felt sorry for the stallholder who was inside the cordon. No doubt that would be the end of his trading for the day. Frederick watched him pack his things away, filling boxes.

Not long after the cordon went up, a forensics team arrived to set up a tent, and Horace had told Frederick he was escorting Christina and Mary Anne back to Marjorie's. Frederick noticed the uniformed officer who had been speaking to the doctor had been replaced by a grumpy-looking detective. He leaned in closer to hear what was being said.

"Are you sure?"

"I couldn't swear to it, but the man carried two adrenaline auto injectors on his person and his face matched someone who had suffered anaphylaxis. By the time I found the injectors, it was too late."

"And you think whatever killed him was in the food?"

"Again, Detective, I can't be certain, but that's the most likely explanation."

Frederick's heart leapt. Marjorie had been right about the food causing Marcus's death, but mistaken about poisoning. If Marcus had died as the result of an allergy, it was more than likely an accidental death, so the housekeeper would be off the hook.

Frederick was stunned out of his happy notions when the detective spoke again.

"And is it likely that whoever prepared the deceased's lunch would have known about his allergy?"

"People who carry auto injectors for food allergies are ultra-careful about what they eat. So, almost certainly."

Frederick's heart sank.

At that moment, a large woman arrived carrying a medical bag. She donned white coveralls and overshoes before the police removed the cordon for her. The woman's round face had a weatherworn look and a double chin rested on her ample chest. She nodded to the person who had set up the tent.

"About time too!" the detective snapped.

"Good to see you too, DI Crow," said the woman, placing her bag on the floor, breathless from the exertion of pulling on coveralls that were too small for her. Frederick assumed she was the pathologist.

"I suppose you had to finish the eighteenth hole."

Frederick tried to imagine the woman hitting a golf ball and decided she would probably drive it a long way. He couldn't work out whether the inspector was joking or was truly annoyed. His face was deadpan.

The woman chortled. "I was playing with the commissioner, so watch yourself, Corbin. Now, what have we got here?"

Frederick watched as the inspector called Corbin Crow showed her a driving licence in a plastic bag. "Sixty-year-old male Caucasian collapsed after eating a sandwich. Name of Marcus Singleton. This is Doctor Stacy Parker, who tried to resuscitate the man while waiting for an ambulance. She's the one who called us in and confirmed death. We gathered what we could while trying to keep people back. The CSI team arrived not long ago. He's in there." The detective inclined his head towards the tent.

The woman nodded at Dr Parker. "Sorry, I can't shake hands. I'm Brenda Stamp, north London pathologist. I take it you think the dead man was poisoned?"

Stacy Parker shook her head. "Anaphylactic shock. I was just telling Inspector Crow the dead man carried two auto injectors."

"So why am I here?" Brenda Stamp shot an angry look at Corbin Crow.

"Because, Doctor Stamp, he didn't buy his food here. Someone prepared his lunch. And the sandwich bag had his name written on it." The detective's tone was triumphant.

"And so, you chose to go in for overkill. Let me get this straight: you've disrupted trading at a very busy Christmas market, attracting unnecessary publicity to the scene, and expect me to look at a body in the freezing cold when I could do all this – and more – back at the mortuary."

Crow's face reddened before recovering. "Just a quick look if you don't mind, Doctor, and then you can cut him up in your dark domain." The sarcastic detective turned to the doctor who had reported the potential crime. "Thank you, Dr Parker. If we need to call you, we know where you are." Having dismissed one doctor and insisted another one stay, Inspector Crow spun around on his heels and walked over to one of the uniformed officers who was holding a pad and marking people in and out. "Keep the gawkers away, will you?"

Before deciding it was time to move on, Frederick heard the pathologist, Brenda Stamp, bemoaning her lot to one of the CSI team. "Now I'm here, I might as well look. You never know, we might unravel the crime of the century."

Frederick returned to the food square and watched the *crime* scene from there, nestling his hands around a mug of hot coffee. The pathologist didn't hang about for long and the CSIs removed the body and tent in quick succession once she was satisfied there was no need to further disrupt trading. The stallholder who had been packing away seemed delighted, cheerfully unpacking everything again, and was back to selling as if nothing had happened within thirty minutes. DI Crow left the scene following a brief conversation with Brenda Stamp, and that was the end of it. Death was so final, Frederick mused.

After finishing a second cup of coffee, Frederick eyed Colm McCleary and his mistress Melissa, whose real surname he didn't know, walking arm in arm, chatting happily without a care in the world. Frederick couldn't help feeling sorry for Colm's actual wife. Was she aware her husband had a mistress? It was such an old-fashioned word, Frederick thought, but he couldn't come up with a decent alternative. Girlfriend didn't seem right because Colm already had a wife; partner was hardly appropriate, as the man wasn't separated.

Mistress it will have to be, he decided. Perhaps he'd ask Marjorie what she thought when he got back to the house.

Thoughts of Marjorie always brought a warm feeling to his heart. He admired her immensely; she was sharp, witty and elegant and had become a dear friend. Who was he trying to kid? His heart longed for more than friendship: a companion to spend his later years with. Although he still missed his late wife, Marjorie had brought back the spark of youth to his heart. Was it right to have such longings at his age?

"Age is just a number," his wife used to say, and she was right. Having a soulmate again would be so fulfilling, but he had to accept that Marjorie wanted to keep things as they were, despite him suspecting she had feelings for him too. It was certainly less complicated that way, and he felt privileged to have her close friendship.

"Do you mind if I join you?"

Frederick looked up to see a young woman with wavy black hair looking at him through saucerlike brown eyes. She was beautiful and reminded him of his daughter-in-law.

"I was just leaving," he said, finishing his drink.

"It won't take long, sir."

The *sir* drew his attention to the identity card she slid across the table.

"I'm sorry," he said, "I thought… never mind what I thought. What can I do for you, Detective Sergeant Owlowpis?"

Maria Ouloupis smiled, putting her card back in her handbag, and took the bench opposite. "It's pronounced Ooloopees. I was wondering if I could have a word about what you witnessed earlier. A stallholder told me you had an altercation with a man just before he collapsed and died."

Frederick felt sweat forming beneath his hat before it trickled down his temples. He fidgeted with the brim of his hat, but didn't dare remove it, even though the wool rubbed against his clammy skin. He felt his face redden. *Why do the police always make people feel guilty?*

"It wasn't exactly an altercation. Marcus had yelled at my, erm… friend Marjorie."

"You knew the deceased, sir?" He had inadvertently piqued Detective Ouloupis's interest. She took out her notebook.

"No. Not really. We met yesterday. He's an employee of my friend's son. Marjorie is hosting guests for the week while they do business with her son." Frederick was stumbling over his words, but couldn't stop himself.

"Does your friend Marjorie have a surname?" The detective looked serious, but her eyes were smiling.

"Snellthorpe. Lady Marjorie Snellthorpe, and her son is Lord Jeremy Snellthorpe, although he doesn't use the title very often." *Too much information,* he told himself.

"So, the deceased man was also a guest in Lady Snellthorpe's home?"

"A day guest. He wasn't staying overnight."

"Did Lady Snellthorpe prepare lunches for the guests?"

"No!" Frederick cleared his throat, realising he had raised his voice, sounding defensive. Detective Ouloupis wrote notes on her pad. He couldn't read them, as her handwriting was worse than his wife's had been.

Occupational hazard, he thought.

"And your name, sir?"

"Frederick Mackworth. I'm staying at Marjorie's, Detective Owl… loopees. She prefers to be called Marjorie," he added.

"Got it. You can call me Maria. People struggle with the surname, although it's not that difficult."

"Is it Greek?"

"Greek Cypriot. My parents are from Nicosia, but I was born and bred in London. You could probably tell that from the accent."

"It is rather cockney."

"Where's yours from?"

"I'm from the West Country." Maria had put him at ease. His heart was slowing down.

"So, who prepared Mr Singleton's lunch?"

"Marjorie's son has brought a temporary cook in because the usual one's on holiday. I assume she prepared the lunches." Frederick pinched his thigh, as if punishing himself for not being totally honest.

"And did the cook hand out the lunches her or himself?"

"The cook is she, but no, she didn't. Temporary staff hired for the week brought the lunch packs to the front door."

Maria scribbled in her notebook again before chewing the end of her pen. She had immaculately manicured fingernails, although they weren't painted. Her olive skin was smooth, with no makeup.

"Could you tell me more about the row?"

The question jolted Frederick away from his thoughts. "What row?"

"The confrontation, then."

"With Marcus?"

Maria nodded.

"It was nothing, really. Marjorie accidentally bumped into him and he rounded on her. She's only just over five feet and I suppose you know how tall he was, so I stood between them and told him there was no need to shout."

"Is that all?"

"Yes. The next thing, he collapsed. I couldn't feel a pulse and I heard someone calling an ambulance, then a doctor came along. We assumed he'd had a heart attack."

"Is that everything?"

"It is," said Frederick.

"What about him taking a big bite of his lunch? Did you not see that?"

Frederick felt himself redden. "I did. Sorry, I forgot to say."

"And Marjorie's bumping into him. Are you certain that was an accident?"

"Of course. What are you suggesting?"

"Just asking questions, sir. It's what I do."

Frederick removed a handkerchief from his pocket and mopped his brow. "Please call me Frederick."

"Would you mind writing the address where you're staying, Frederick?"

Frederick did as asked, and then watched Maria Ouloupis when she left for another chat with the stallholder. She had her notebook out while asking him a few more questions. What on earth were the police thinking? Surely they couldn't imagine Marjorie had anything to do with Marcus Singleton's death?

He stood up, almost falling over the bench in his hurry to get away. Frederick felt Maria's eyes boring into the back of his head. He knew he was making a hash of things and she would think he had something to hide.

"Are you heading back?"

Bruce startled Frederick, appearing at his side.

"Yes, I am," he said, increasing his pace.

Bruce kept pace with him as he raced through the growing crowds coming for the evening. "Are we late for something?" Bruce asked.

"No. I've had enough, that's all."

"Ah. Is it the Marcus thing sinking in? Elmur's been going on about it all afternoon, but, hey… we've all got to go someday, and that was a nice way to go."

Frederick couldn't quite believe his ears. Did no-one care about Marcus Singleton's death?

"Do you know if he was married?" He blurted out the question, wondering why he hadn't asked it before.

"Divorced, I think. I expect the police will have contacted his next of kin. Elmur didn't think he had any children, though. What are the police doing here?"

"Presumably they are called to all sudden deaths."

"I don't think they are, but I'm no expert. Who was that gorgeous-looking woman you were talking to just now? Family?"

Frederick was digging himself into a hole he didn't know how to get out of and all for no reason.

"Do you want to share a taxi?"

"Makes sense. Colm and his bit of stuff left earlier."

"What about Elmur?"

"He's too busy gambling."

They climbed into a taxi, and Frederick gave the driver the address. Bruce was turning out to be an irritating gossip, but Marjorie would want to know what he'd found out.

"I didn't see any bookmakers around here."

"Not that sort of gambling. He's betting on currency trading on his phone. He showed me what it was, but it looked too high risk for me. I like to keep my money secure. Anyway, by the strain on his face, he looked like he was losing big time. A friend of mine used to be into that sort of thing and went bankrupt. You can lose thousands in minutes if you bet the wrong way, and the more you try to get your money back, the more you lose."

"And I thought having the odd bet on the horses was bad enough," said Frederick.

"I think Elmur's got it bad, if I'm honest. I only asked about it to see if I could divert him from his phone, but then when I succeeded, all he did was go on about Marcus's death. Quite animated, he was. I don't think he was sorry to see him go."

"What makes you say that?" They were almost back at Marjorie's, and Frederick wanted to know whether anything Bruce was saying was relevant.

"They didn't get on. Marcus was brutal enough to find out our weaknesses – mine's women, by the way – and trust me, if Elmur's gambling is more than a hobby, Marcus would have tried to exploit it."

The taxi pulled up outside Marjorie's. The two men split the fare, and Frederick gave the driver a tip. No sooner had they got out of the taxi than another one drew up. An angry-looking Elmur Cartwright alighted from the vehicle.

"Didn't you hear me? I was calling you to wait."

Chapter 12

"I suppose I'd better see how Sally's doing with dinner," said Marjorie, finishing her toddy.

Before she had the opportunity to leave the room, Frederick burst through the door, almost knocking her over. He was flushed and breathless and still wearing his hat and overcoat.

"What on earth's happened?" Edna asked.

"Where's Marjorie?"

"Flattened against the wall. You almost knocked her down," said Horace.

Frederick's head swung around ninety degrees, eyes wide with horror.

"Ignore him. I'm all right, but what is the matter?"

Frederick threw himself into a chair. "Just let me get my breath back a minute."

"Take your coat off, man, and you'll be less hot," said Edna, impatience getting the better of her.

Horace took Frederick's hat and coat and headed to the door as Elsa walked in.

"Let me take those," she offered and Horace obliged. "I just came to tell you that dinner will be ready at eight-thirty. Sally wants to know if drinks and canapés are needed beforehand."

"It might be worth having a few things set up in the reception room in case people want to mingle in there before dinner," said Marjorie.

Elsa caught sight of Frederick and raised an eyebrow. "Should I bring anything through here?"

"No, thank you. We'll help ourselves from the cabinet."

"I'll collect the tray later," Elsa said, shooting another quizzical glance Frederick's way.

"Thank you," Marjorie said, returning to a seat herself.

After Elsa had left, Edna poured Frederick a brandy from the drinks cabinet.

"Want one, Marge?"

"No thank you."

Edna shrugged, filling whisky glasses with Scotch for herself and Horace. They waited for Frederick to compose himself.

Finally, he spoke. "It wasn't poison, it was an anaphylactic reaction."

"Well, that's good news," said Edna. "It means Mrs Ratton's off the hook."

Frederick shook his head vigorously. "No. The police suspect someone deliberately put the allergen in his lunch. I heard them discussing it. What's worse, a detective interviewed me."

"Oh dear. Did they catch you eavesdropping? I hope you didn't mention Mrs Ratton," Marjorie said.

"No, I didn't. But it won't be long before they find out who prepared his lunch, otherwise suspicion will go onto the cook. They even asked if you prepared lunch, Marjorie."

Edna snorted.

"Maria's not stupid."

"Maria?" asked Horace.

"Maria Ouloupis; she's the detective. She asked me for your address, Marjorie. She asked if the cook gave him the lunch herself and I told her that other people brought the lunches out from the kitchen. I expect she'll want to interview the temporary staff as well."

"At least it means they won't be able to prove Gina Ratton did what they say. Anyone could have slipped the substance into his sandwich pack. I don't believe Gina had anything to do with this," Marjorie said.

"I didn't know anything about him being allergic to anything," said Edna. "He seemed to throw whatever he could get hold of down his throat. Him and Elmur were similar in that way."

"That might have been the only thing those two had in common," said Frederick.

"Did he even tell anyone he had allergies?" Edna was not to be put off.

"You make a good point, Edna," said Marjorie. "I wasn't aware of any, and I'm head of this household."

"Yeah, but you're hardly head of the cooking, are you, Marge?" said Edna.

"Nevertheless, I would need to know. Gloria would have told me."

"I'm confused; I thought the cook's name is Sally Sutherland," said Horace.

"Gloria's my usual cook, and she briefed Sally before she left. Although…" Marjorie rubbed her head, "that was before Gloria knew about the existence of Marcus Singleton, let alone that he would end up hanging around, making everyone feel uncomfortable. I wonder if he told Sally himself. I think they met."

"In which case, Sally might not have thought to mention it to you, or she assumed you knew," Horace suggested.

"Either way, Marcus's death is likely to be an accident after all," said Edna. "Sally probably forgot to tell Mrs

Ratton about his allergy. Did your Maria friend say what he was allergic to? It's usually nuts."

Frederick shook his head. "She didn't say. I'm not sure she knew. The only reason they decided it was anaphylaxis at all is because the doctor who attended him found adrenaline pens on his person."

"Are they those anti-allergic syringe things?" Edna asked.

"Yes, filled with adrenaline for emergency use," said Frederick.

"This could work in Gina's favour," said Horace. "At worst, it was neglect, or a poor joke if Sally deliberately withheld the information, perhaps not realising what the consequences could be."

"You're right," said Marjorie, "although it would be an extremely dangerous thing to do as a joke. Let's hope it was an oversight."

Frederick put his head in his hands. "There's something else." His grey eyes implored Marjorie to look at him and she did.

"What?"

"Maria – the detective sergeant – said the stallholder told her I had a row with Marcus just before he died."

"That's ridiculous," Marjorie snapped. "It was hardly a row."

"What's this? You mentioned nothing about an argument," Edna said.

"It slipped my mind because it wasn't an argument and after Marcus collapsed and died, our thoughts were otherwise occupied."

"Maria was very nice, but I think she might have got the wrong impression about it. I'm not very good at these things. The police intimidate me."

"Don't we know it," said Edna. "I remember when you incriminated yourself in Romania, when all you had to do was tell the truth. I hope you didn't lie to her. It'll come back to haunt you if you did." She glared at Frederick.

Frederick wiped sweat from his forehead, eyes darting from one to the other.

"Tell us what happened," said Marjorie gently.

"Maria asked who prepared Marcus's lunch, and I told her you had hired a new cook. I didn't exactly say she was the one."

"Seriously?" Edna snapped. "Some people never learn."

"Other than that, I told the truth, but even that sounded bad the way I said it."

"What do you mean?" Horace asked.

"This argument that wasn't an argument. I was trying to explain to Maria how I intervened because Marcus shouted at Marjorie after she bumped into him. That's all that happened, but it sounded worse in retrospect. Anyway, I forgot to mention Marcus biting the sandwich, and she pulled me up on it. She asked me if Marjorie bumped into Marcus on purpose and I sounded defensive. Now I think she suspects I was covering up for you, Marjorie, or colluding."

Marjorie felt her eyes widen. "You're not suggesting the police think I had anything to do with his death?"

Frederick wrung his hands. "They might."

Horace sipped his Scotch before saying, "I can see how they might imagine that from what Fred's told us, but let's face it: you don't have a motive, Marjorie. It won't take long to clear this up."

"Precisely," said Marjorie, feeling guilty for having been pleased Marcus Singleton wouldn't be darkening her door again.

"Unless they find one," said Horace.

Edna burst out laughing, and everyone looked at her. "Sorry, Marge, but I'm just picturing PC Plod taking you away in handcuffs and the headlines in the *Hampstead Gazette*: 'Death by Sandwich: Late Peer's wife, Lady Marjorie Snellthorpe, arrested after providing one sandwich too many!'" Edna snorted.

Marjorie could see the funny side and chuckled, adding, "Assisted by her avaricious cousin-in-law and an ex-pharmacist."

"This is serious," said Frederick. "I can imagine Maria doing background checks as we speak. What if she finds out how death follows you around, Marjorie, and twists everything? She might reopen investigations and turn you into a serial killer."

Horace patted Frederick on the shoulder. "You're letting your imagination run away with you, old chap. If that were the case, we'd all be implicated. Now calm down, Fred, there's nothing for them to find. Let them do their checks. What we need to concentrate on is what went into the sandwiches and who put it there if we're going to clear Marjorie's housekeeper."

"But what if the police question Marjorie?" Frederick's voice sounded shaky.

"She'll handle it a damn sight better than you did, that's for sure," said Edna, regaining her composure after her giggling interlude.

"There's something else I found out," said Frederick.

"Don't tell us: Marjorie's arranged for poisoned truffles for dessert this evening and we're all goners." Edna burst into a giggling fit again. Horace couldn't help joining her in what ended up as a joint snorting session.

"I'd like to hear what else you discovered, Frederick, even if these two wouldn't," said Marjorie.

Edna and Horace composed themselves again and looked expectantly at Frederick.

"Bruce told me Elmur might be losing a lot of money betting on the currency markets and Marcus might have known about it. If he did, Bruce reckons he would have exploited the fact."

"Mm, not much of a motive for murder," said Horace.

"Unless he's keeping a gambling addiction from his wife and stealing or borrowing money to feed it," said Marjorie.

"It would explain the summons to see Marcus this morning," Edna added.

"You're right," said Horace. "What if Marcus was using blackmail to get the deal at rock-bottom prices? Mary Anne intimated he wasn't above doing dodgy deals to get what he wanted."

"But would Elmur have known about the man's allergy?" Edna said.

"I wouldn't have thought so, unless someone told him about it. Who hired Sally Sutherland?" Horace asked.

"Jeremy," said Marjorie. "And although he sounded relieved that Marcus was out of the way as he was becoming a liability, I don't believe my son is a killer. Neither would he put that sort of pressure on a negotiator to get a deal."

"I wonder if Marcus might have been doing some side deals for himself," Horace said.

"So, we're back to Mrs Ratton," said Edna, "who Marjorie couldn't bring herself to ask how she knew Marcus Singleton and why she might want to kill him."

They heard footsteps in the hallway. "Sounds like the guests are down," said Horace.

Marjorie stood. "I suggest we go in and see what we can glean from them, particularly Elmur, Mary Anne and Christina. They all have things to hide, I'm sure of it, and one of those things might be a motive for murder. I'll also have a word with Sally after dinner about any special dietary needs and allergies she knows about regarding the guests, see what she has to say. If she knew about his allergy and told Gina about it, I promise I'll speak to Gina tomorrow. She'll have gone home by now."

"Right, team. Let's go," said Horace.

"When do you think the police will be knocking at the door?" Edna asked.

"I'm expecting them to turn up some time this evening," said Marjorie. "It could make for an interesting dinner. Will Faith be joining us tonight?"

"No," said Horace. "She'll be here first thing to take the group to see the sights."

"Right then. Here goes." Marjorie performed an imaginary rolling up of the sleeves before leading her friends from the lounge to the reception room. A large picture of horses galloping across a beach, dominating the main wall, seemed appropriate for the moment.

Another original, she thought. *Marcus Singleton would have liked that.* There was something else playing at the back of her mind, but she couldn't quite bring it to the fore. She felt it might be significant, but sometimes things were annoyingly blurred in the recesses of her brain. If only she could summon them at will. No doubt it would come to her in the middle of the night, unbidden. Whatever it was, it could provide the answer to Marcus Singleton's death.

Chapter 13

Just before dinner was announced, the dreaded sound of the doorbell made Marjorie shiver. She turned to look for her friends who were entertaining the guests, no doubt subtly pressing them for stories of their lives. Marjorie had only just started a conversation with Christina and was building up to enquiring about any past dealings she'd had with Marcus. Not that Christina had owned up to any, but Marjorie knew from what Mary Anne had said that there had been something between them.

Elsa came into the room and tapped her on the shoulder. "The police are here and they want to speak to Sally," she whispered.

"Please excuse me," Marjorie said to Christina. Thankfully, Christina was being distracted by Horace, who had rushed over to help. He gave Marjorie a wink.

Marjorie found a surly round man of medium height with puffy pockmarked cheeks stomping up and down impatiently. He wore an ill-fitting overcoat and the collar of his shirt was frayed at the neck. His tie hung loosely and his dirty brown shoes had already left mud stains in the hall.

Elsa made the introductions. "This is Detective Inspector Corbin Crow…" Marjorie was pleased Edna wasn't there or she would have burst out laughing, "….and Detective Sergeant Maria Ouloupis. This is Lady Marjorie Snellthorpe."

"Thank you, Elsa. We'll let you get on."

"I need to speak to your cook," Corbin Crow barked.

"Good evening to you, Inspector. I'm afraid Sally is about to serve dinner for a large number of guests. Perhaps you could come through to my sitting room while we wait."

The detective appeared flustered, as if not used to not getting his own way. He brushed a mop of a fringe away from his eyes before clearing his throat.

"Well, erm…"

"We wanted to speak to Lady Marjorie as well, sir," the more amicable-looking Maria Ouloupis said. Marjorie could see why she had unsettled Frederick. She had a disarming air, with a penetrating gaze which focused through attractive round eyes.

"Oh yes. I suppose we could. If we're not dragging you away from your extinguished guests." The sarcasm might have been effective if the inspector had chosen the right word. Under the circumstances, it was rather inappropriate, as one of her guests had indeed been extinguished.

"My *distinguished* guests can wait, Inspector. Please, come this way."

Corbin Crow had a flat pug nose. Had it been pointed, he could well have been a crow, except they are intelligent creatures and she didn't know yet whether Inspector Crow matched up. Still, Marjorie wouldn't underestimate the DI; his word slip-up could have been a ruse.

Once they were in the sitting room, the inspector paced the floor. DS Ouloupis took the seat Marjorie indicated.

"May I offer you a drink?"

"We're on duty," Crow growled. For such a young man, Marjorie guessed late thirties, he was far too officious.

"I have soda water, lemonade, even tap water."

"Okay. I'll have lemonade."

No manners either, she mused. "With ice?"

"What? Yes, yes." He waved a hand at her to get on with it.

"And for you, Sergeant Ouloupis?"

DS Ouloupis grinned while taking out a notebook from her pocket. "I'll have a soda water, please."

Once she had poured the drinks and handed them out, Marjorie took a seat. Inspector Crow ignored her, continuing to wear down her rug while blocking heat from the open fire.

"You said you wanted to ask me some questions. I assume this is about the unfortunate death of Mr Singleton?" Marjorie addressed DS Ouloupis.

"Yes, it is. A Mr Mackworth told me he was a guest of yours."

"Not quite. Mr Singleton was an employee of my son's and was here to negotiate a deal with suppliers. The suppliers are all houseguests, you see, but Jeremy – that's my son – had arranged for Marcus to meet with them both formally and informally."

DS Ouloupis wrote quickly.

"So, you've known the deceased for some time?" Crow broke in.

"I'm afraid not, Inspector. My son brought him here yesterday, and that was the first time I had set eyes on him."

"We understand you bumped into him at the market. It has been suggested that might have been deliberate." Crow made it sound more like an accusation than a suggestion.

Marjorie chuckled. "Why on earth would I do such a thing? Marcus towered over me. Not to mention, if you had met him, you would know he wasn't the kind of man one would barge into. It hurt me more than it did him, I can assure you."

"And yet your friend, Mr Mackworth, felt you needed protection." Corbin Crow scrunched his forehead.

"Only because Marcus was a short-tempered man and started yelling. It's not the sort of behaviour either of us is used to, but once Marcus recognised us, he realised his mistake and calmed down, taking his temper out on his lunch rather than me. I'm sure your source would have told you this."

Maria's smile lit up her face. She was so different from her boss. A case of good cop, bad cop.

"He did. We just wanted to hear it from your side."

"And now you want to know if I deliberately slipped an allergen into his sandwich during this brief interaction?" Marjorie said.

"How did you know about that?" Inspector Crow barked.

Lady Marjorie was tempted to ask if he and Singleton were related, as they had a similar manner, but instead she said, "You were overheard, Inspector. You have a rather loud voice." Marjorie kept her steely eyes on him, but noticed in her peripheral vision that DS Ouloupis's lips turned upwards.

"Hmm. Anyway. That's what we thought… well, that's what the doctor thought."

Marjorie waited for him to go on, but he didn't.

"Was that the pleasant young doctor who tried to save him? Unless I'm mistaken, he carried allergy injections."

"Yes, but not for a food allergy. He was allergic to bee stings and we don't get many of them around in December," the

shot back.

Marjorie was confused and sorry she had riled him, but she needed answers, so she would persevere. "Oh dear. At least that explains why Sally didn't mention any food allergies. You mean it was a heart attack after all?" she asked.

Corbin Crow cast his narrowed tan-brown eyes her way. "No, Mrs Snellthorpe. He was poisoned."

"Please, call me Marjorie or Lady Snellthorpe, Inspector. My husband died some years ago and I was never known as Mrs, even when we were married."

"Noted," said the DI.

"That's why we need to speak to your cook," DS Ouloupis explained. "Did you say her name is Sally?"

"Yes, Sally Sutherland. But I think you already know that, Sergeant."

"And she's temping for you this week? What else do you know about her?"

"Other than she is an excellent cook and has a dog called Hercules, nothing. My son hired her through an agency when I told him my cook would be on holiday."

DS Ouloupis scribbled notes down on her pad. "Is your son here?"

"No. He had a longstanding engagement and won't be here until tomorrow evening."

"Even though his negotiator is dead?"

"My son was sorry to hear of Mr Singleton's demise, but as far as he knows, the man died from an allergic reaction or a heart attack. These things happen, Inspector."

"How long will this Sally woman be? We haven't got all night," said Inspector Crow.

"If you're hungry, Inspector, I can arrange for a tray."

DS Ouloupis smirked. "It might be a good idea, sir."

"I don't need food. I need to speak to the cook."

"Her name's Sally," said Marjorie. "Perhaps I can help you. What kind of poison was it?"

"How can you knowing that help us?" DI Crow was becoming even more irritable.

DS Ouloupis got what Marjorie was inferring. "Do you have any potassium cyanide in the house?"

"Oh my word; cyanide poisoning. We used to have some in the shed, but that was many years ago when it was a common way to get rid of wasps' nests. The only poison we had in the shed more recently was rat poison, but I don't even think we have that anymore. I asked the gardener not to use it. It's such a cruel way to kill vermin, despite its effectiveness."

The DI let out a heavy sigh before rolling his eyes.

He's such a rude man, thought Marjorie. At that moment, Edna came in.

"Elsa told me you were waiting for Sally. Dinner's being served now, so she'll be free in about fifteen minutes."

"And you are?" Inspector Crow snapped.

"Edna Parkinton. Marge's cousin…" Marjorie noticed a crinkle around the DI's eyes. "What about you?"

"This is Detective Inspector Corbin Crow…" Edna spluttered, but Marjorie continued, "… and this is Detective Sergeant Maria Ouloupis."

"Good pronunciation, Marjorie. I'm impressed."

"My late husband and I spent a lot of time in the Greek part of Cyprus and knew a family out there with the same surname."

DS Ouloupis smiled. "Please, feel free to call me Maria."

Inspector Crow rolled his eyes again.

"What about you, Inspector Corbin Crow? Where did you fly in from?" asked Edna.

The DI's face turned puce before he surprised them all by grinning at Edna. "I've heard that joke a thousand times, Mrs… or is it Lady Parkinton?"

"Edna to you," she said, causing the DI to laugh out loud. Maria appeared to be as surprised as Marjorie was. How did Edna do it?

"I hail from your parts, Edna. Lancashire, is it?"

"Yes. You see, Marge, us northerners stick together. Anyway, have you told him?"

"Told me what?" A less friendly face turned towards Marjorie.

"I was just about to. Apparently Edna, Marcus Singleton was poisoned and I think the inspector suspects the cook." She turned to face Maria. "Sally didn't prepare Marcus's lunch."

"Then who did?"

"I did." Marjorie did not know why she said it, but the words tumbled out of her mouth before she could stop them.

Edna's mouth opened wide, and then closed again.

"I see," said DI Crow.

"And did you have any reason to poison Marcus Singleton?" Maria asked.

"No, Sergeant… Maria, I didn't. As I said, we met for the first time yesterday. He was a rather unpleasant man, but if I poisoned all the unpleasant men I came across, I'd be serving a long prison sentence." Marjorie fixed her eyes on Inspector Crow to make her point.

"And did you also fill his flask?" Maria asked, suppressing a grin.

"I thought the poison was in his sandwich?" said Marjorie.

"No, the poison was in his drink. Answer the question. Did you prepare that too?" DI Crow looked at her sceptically.

"Guilty," she said, crossing her fingers behind her back.

"This, of course, means we're going to have to interview everyone who had access to the man's flask. Including your *distinguished* guests, Lady Marjorie." DI Crow had gained the upper hand, and he knew it.

"Tonight?"

"Yes, tonight." He looked around the sitting room. "Perhaps we could use this room for our interviews, if it wouldn't be too much trouble," he said. "And I'd still like to start with the cook."

"You can use the library, Inspector. There's a desk in there and it's more private. We wouldn't want you to be overheard again, would we?"

Maria tried and failed to hide another smirk.

Chapter 14

Once the police were safely ensconced in the library with Sally Sutherland as the first interviewee, Marjorie was on her way to tell the guests that the police would be speaking to them when she heard something.

"Psst… in here." Edna was still in the small sitting room, holding the door ajar. Marjorie looked around before answering the summons, but couldn't see what she was hiding from.

"Is there something the matter?"

Edna almost pulled her into the room. "What the heck are you doing, Marge? You can't just lie to the police like that."

"I didn't mean to lie, it just slipped out. I couldn't have them banging on Gina's door at this time of night. Besides, it's bought us some time, hasn't it?" Marjorie smiled, feeling pleased with herself.

Edna's look was grim. "You'll be doing time if you're not careful. This is now a murder inquiry, Marge, and you've just done that thing called perverting the course of justice… that's a crime, you know?"

"Oh dear, I hadn't thought of it like that. I'm sure when I explain, Inspector Crow will understand."

"Don't bet on it," said Edna. "He didn't take to you. Northerners aren't impressed by all this la-di-da stuff and people like Corbin Crow…" Edna spluttered with a slight giggle "… would be happy to take you down a peg. Make an example of you and all that."

Marjorie felt lightheaded. She reached for the back of the sofa.

"I've made a bit of a hash of things, haven't I?"

"You could say that," said Edna. "Not only that, though, you've made it look like you're hiding something and your housekeeper will seem more guilty in their eyes once they find out you lied. Are you all right? You look as though you're going to pass out."

Marjorie shook her head. "I just feel a bit queasy, that's all. It's been an eventful day. I was only trying to protect Gina. You would have done the same thing."

Concern filled Edna's eyes, and she strolled over to the drinks cabinet. "Sit down for a minute. Let's get you a brandy."

After a few sips, Marjorie felt better. "I really must ask the guests to stay around if they are going to be interviewed by the police. Did you say they had started dinner?"

"They should have by now. I think it's best not to mention why the police want to talk to them. I don't want you telling any more lies," said Edna.

Normally Marjorie would offer a retort, but she could see that Edna was concerned rather than sniping.

By the time Marjorie and Edna arrived in the dining room, everyone had finished dinner. On seeing the two women, they brought their chattering to an abrupt halt.

"Have they gone?" Colm asked.

"Who?" Marjorie replied.

"The police. Elsa told us the police were here."

Marjorie's lips tightened. She really must have a word with Elsa.

"They are still here, I'm afraid. They say Mr Singleton was poisoned…" Edna glared at her for ignoring her advice but she continued, "… and they would like to interview everyone. When we've finished in here, we should move through to the other room."

Murmuring spread around the table as the news sank in. Marjorie couldn't help wondering if the killer was in this room. As the guests started to move, Horace and Frederick hung back until they had all gone through to the reception room, where their chattering became louder.

"Poison?" Horace was the first to speak.

"Yes," said Marjorie.

"Not an anaphylactic reaction, then?" Frederick asked.

"No. Apparently he was allergic to bee stings, which is why none of us knew about any food allergies. Someone put the poison in his flask."

"But why are they interviewing us and not Mrs Ratton? Sorry, Marjorie, I know she's your housekeeper, but she must be their prime suspect," Horace said.

"Tell him, Marge," said Edna, folding her arms.

"Keep your voice down," said Marjorie. After checking to make sure no-one was in the vicinity, she lowered her own voice. "The police believe I prepared his lunch."

"Why on earth would they think that?" Frederick asked. "I told them you didn't prepare the food. Let me put them straight." He took a step towards the door.

Marjorie reached out, touching his arm. "It's my doing. The inspector pressed me and I couldn't think of anything else to say. I thought it would give us time to plan the next steps."

Frederick's eyes widened. "You lied to the police?"

"Don't you come all high and mighty, Mister," Edna leapt to Marjorie's defence. "You hardly have an exemplary track record in the truth-to-the-cops department. If you'd told them who prepared lunch in the first place, we wouldn't be in this position, would we?"

Frederick flushed red, his bald head shining under the light of the chandelier.

"Settle down, everyone," said Horace. "What's done is done. They might understand once they know the truth, but for now, Marjorie's right. Our focus should be on that lot next door." He inclined his head towards the doors separating the dining room from the reception room. "Where are the police now?"

"In the library," said Marjorie, "interviewing Sally."

"Who do you think they'll speak to next?" Horace asked.

"Elsa, I would have thought, and then the waiting staff who brought the lunches from the kitchen this morning. Are they still here?"

"Yes. I think they went to help Elsa. They'll be back to clear this lot up soon. You also need to eat something, Marjorie," said Frederick. "You don't look well."

"I'm fine. I will get something to eat when the police are out of my house."

"Perhaps you had better have a word with Elsa before the police do," said Horace.

"I can't ask her to lie for me."

"No. But you can ask her not to mention your housekeeper for now unless she absolutely has to. There would be no reason for the plods to think Gina Ratton was anywhere near the lunches, unless someone mentions it," said Edna.

Marjorie's hand covered her mouth. "Elsa may not know who prepared lunch for Marcus, but Sally does and she's in with them now."

"In which case, we don't have any time to lose. You speak to Elsa anyway and we'll see what we can find out in there," said Horace, already moving towards the reception room. Edna followed him, shaking her head and tutting about them all going to jail.

Frederick patted Marjorie on the arm. "If it's any consolation, I would have done the same if it was one of mine. When I ran the pharmacy, the staff became like family. We would have done anything for each other. Your instincts are good, Marjorie. Mrs Ratton has done nothing wrong, so let's find out who has, shall we?"

"Thank you," she said, feeling better.

Frederick left her to join the others, and she took a moment to steel herself before moving into the hallway.

The library door opened and Inspector Crow marched out with a smug grin on his face. "You can tell your guests we won't be interviewing them after all," he said.

Horror followed Marjorie's delight when Maria and a red-faced Sally exited the library. "What's going on, Inspector?" Marjorie quizzed.

"Miss Sutherland is accompanying us to the station. Helping us with our inquiries," he said before leaning in close. "You really shouldn't tell porkies, *Lady* Marjorie."

Marjorie felt her mouth twitching. "But, Inspector, I told you Sally didn't—"

Sally shook her head. "Would you mind feeding Hercules until I get back?"

"I don't know where his food is," Marjorie said. "Inspector, do you mind if Sally shows me?"

"Who the heck's Hercules?"

"The dog, sir," said Maria.

"Hurry up about it," he snapped. "We've wasted enough time already. I've got better things to do than be given the runaround by... by..." DI Crow stopped himself before he said anything too rude.

Marjorie found it difficult to keep up with Sally, who was on a mission. To her dismay, Maria followed them. Sally showed her a plastic crate filled with dried food and picked up a scoop.

"He has two of these in the evening and one in the morning. You add cold water to it. Sorry about this," she said.

"You have nothing to be sorry for. I don't understand."

They heard Inspector Crow's heavy footsteps heading their way, which distracted Maria for a moment. Sally took Marjorie's hand.

"I'll be okay," she whispered. "I know Gina didn't do it. Elsa told me you're good at sleuthing. Find out who really did it."

Marjorie watched, dumbfounded, as the police left the house with her temporary cook. Hercules appeared at her side, letting out a low whine. She patted his head.

"Don't worry, Hercules. She's done nothing wrong." Marjorie didn't understand what had just happened, but she was more determined than ever to find a killer, whatever the cost.

Chapter 15

The guests were hanging around, waiting to be called in to see the police, so Marjorie put them out of their misery via Horace. She explained briefly what had happened and asked him to let the guests have the good news that the police wouldn't be interviewing them, without going into detail.

Horace called them all to attention using a spoon against his glass. "You'll be pleased to hear the police have called it a night. They won't be speaking to us after all, so please enjoy the rest of your evening."

A few people exchanged mutterings, but soon returned to their conversations, seemingly in no hurry to leave. Marjorie set about mingling. Edna and Frederick fired quizzical looks in her direction, but she motioned for them to continue what they were doing.

With a determined setting of her jaw, Marjorie joined Christina and Mary Anne. "I am sorry about the confusion," she said. "I think the police have decided to throw their weight around elsewhere."

"Don't tell me, they've arrested the cook." Christina cackled, almost spilling the liquid from her glass.

Mary Anne frowned. "I hope that doesn't mean no breakfast in the morning."

Christina didn't realise how close she was to the truth and Marjorie hadn't given the next day's meals a thought. Horace was sure to have an idea later.

She gave a polite laugh. "Your breakfasts are quite secure, I can assure you. No-one has been arrested. I also wanted to let you know Jeremy is happy to continue negotiations and will join us for dinner tomorrow evening. Our outing into central London is still on, if you would like to go."

"Oh yes, I'm looking forward to it," said Christina. "And good to know we can still do business, despite the not-so-very sad loss of Marcus Singleton."

Mary Anne nudged the other woman. "Shush, Christina. If Marcus was poisoned, you don't want to become a suspect, do you?"

Christina broke her arm free and slurped down the rest of the straw-coloured liquid in her glass. "I need another one of these," she said, stumbling towards the drinks table.

Marjorie wasn't sure whether to ask Horace to make sure Christina would not fall over, but he was otherwise engaged.

"Sorry about her. She's been at the bottle ever since we changed for dinner. I don't think she gets out much these days… since her son—"

"What about her son?" Marjorie asked.

Mary Anne shrugged. "I'm not sure it's for me to say. She told me when we were out, but now she's been blabbing about it all evening, so I suppose it's no secret. If Christina is to be believed, her son used to work for Marcus – not in your son's business, but for an American real estate broker. He was accused of stealing a painting and was fired."

"Who was?"

"Christina's son, Raymond. Anyway, after that, he couldn't get a job anywhere. His father disowned him, and Christina and Raymond argued. He left home and she hasn't seen him since."

"Was Raymond convicted of this crime?"

"No. Marcus persuaded the firm not to press charges, saying it would ruin the boy's chances in life, which I find hard to believe because he was a malicious so-and-so."

"Mm," said Marjorie. "Why is it I get the impression you know more about Marcus Singleton than you let on?

Jeremy told me earlier Marcus had tried to keep you away from the negotiations. Why would he do that?"

"You're right, Marjorie. Marcus and I had history, but it's history I'd rather not talk about. Besides, I think you're needed elsewhere."

Marjorie's eyes followed Mary Anne's. Christina had spilled a drink and Elsa was trying to help the drunken woman out of the room while one of the temporary staff cleared it up.

"Oh dear. Excuse me."

Frederick had just finished talking to Colm and Melissa when she caught his arm. "Would you mind helping with a problem?" She inclined her head towards Christina, who was now sobbing with her arms around Elsa's neck. No-one else seemed to have noticed. Either that or they were being polite and steering clear of the tottering woman.

"You're so kind. My son would like you." Christina was hanging onto Elsa, who was trying not to laugh. Frederick took one arm and Elsa extricated herself from the woman's grasp and took the other.

"Why don't we get you up to bed?" she suggested.

"I'd rather have another one of these." Christina had somehow managed to find an empty glass, which she was likely to drop at any minute. Elsa's eyes pleaded with Marjorie.

"You've had quite enough of those, Mrs Makepeace. Time for bed." Marjorie spoke in as authoritative a tone as she could muster.

"Whoopsie! I'm in the doghouse. Your boss has arrived to send me to bed." Christina's bottom lip stuck out at Elsa like that of a naughty child.

Frederick got the glass safely from Christina's hand and put it on a table. He and Elsa then managed, despite a few stumbles, to get Christina upstairs to her bedroom, followed by Marjorie. Once inside, Christina collapsed on the bed.

Frederick coughed. "Er, I'll leave you to it," he said, blushing.

"Don't go," Christina called. "I haven't had a handsome man take my clothes off for years."

Frederick's face was scarlet.

"That's quite enough of that sort of talk," snapped Marjorie. "Thank you, Frederick. We'll manage from here."

Elsa couldn't help giggling at the speed of Frederick's retreat.

"Frederick. That's a nice name. My husband's name's Hugo… dull name… dull man… what can I say? The only good thing that came from him was our Raymond… and now he's gone." Christina closed her eyes.

"Why don't we get you some coffee and you can tell us all about Raymond? Come along. Sit up."

"You're very bossy, aren't you, Marjorie… or is it Marge?"

"It's Marjorie," she said, firmly. "And you're very drunk."

"I rarely drink, but I'm celebrating." Christina's words were slurred, but she had at least opened her eyes. Elsa fetched a wet flannel from the en suite and handed it to Marjorie.

"I'll get coffee from the pot downstairs. It'll be quicker than going to the kitchen."

"Good idea," said Marjorie. She gently wiped smeared mascara and tears from Christina's eyes, which were puffy and red, with streaks of makeup running down her cheeks. Marjorie gathered up some dribble from her chin.

"Why don't you tell me what it is you are celebrating?"

Christina's eyes suddenly became as black as coal, and her face contorted. She spat the words out.

"The demise of Marcus Singleton. He got what was coming to him."

Elsa arrived with the coffee and the two of them got two mugs of the black liquid down Christina's throat. Once she stopped rambling, Marjorie asked the burning question.

"What did you have against Marcus Singleton?"

Christina waved her arms in the air. "Everything. I had everything against him. He ruined my life. I'd never met him before, but I'd seen photos. When I saw him yesterday, I knew fate had brought us together and I would get my revenge."

Elsa gave a goldfish impression.

"Are you saying you poisoned him?" Marjorie asked.

"No. But tell me who did and I'll buy them a drink. They saved me the job." Christina was becoming more lucid, but now her face was tormented. The sadness in her eyes was pitiful.

"Why did you hate him so much?" Elsa asked.

Christina stared into space. "Because he broke the bond between a mother and her son. I should never have believed it, and I hate myself for it."

Marjorie thought they might go round in circles for ages if she didn't get to the point. "Are you referring to the accusation of theft?"

Christina snapped her head in Marjorie's direction. "You have a son. How would you feel if someone accused him of theft and you believed it?"

"Devastated," said Marjorie honestly.

"Then you know how I feel. Raymond told us again and again that he didn't do it, but we didn't listen. We were more concerned about the damage to our reputation than his. We drove him away."

"Have you tried repairing the relationship?" Marjorie asked.

"I can't. I'm forbidden to contact him. Mr Dull as Ditchwater rules and what he says goes. I might be the MD, but he's in charge."

"It wouldn't stop me contacting my son if I had one," Elsa snapped. The outburst shocked both Marjorie and Christina.

"These things aren't always straightforward," said Marjorie gently.

"They are to me." Elsa's eyes were ablaze. There was obviously more to this story, but now wasn't the time to explore. Marjorie refocused her attention on Christina.

"Tell us what happened."

Christina hesitated, but in the end seemed happy to oblige. "Marcus Singleton, who was then known as Mark Singleton, was an assistant to the director of a real estate company. The senior director had original – and costly – art in every office, according to Raymond. The man liked to flash the cash – to use an expression.

"Anyway, one night, Mark, AKA Marcus, was called to an urgent meeting with a client. He left Raymond finishing up a file for a sale that Marcus told him had to be through the next day and asked him to lock up when he left. Singleton gave him the security code for the building.

"The next morning, when the director got in, there was a blank space on the wall in the boardroom and he called the police. It didn't take long before they accused Raymond of stealing the painting. He phoned me in a desperate state, but when I got to the police station and heard the evidence, it was damning. I told him to come clean and tell them where the painting was. The director offered to drop charges if he returned it. Raymond and I argued; he was devastated I didn't believe him." Christina took a tissue from her sleeve and wiped her eyes.

"What happened next?" Elsa asked.

"Marcus persuaded the director to drop the charges. Raymond was sacked and came home expecting help. Hugo told him to get out. My son looked at me for support, but I turned my head away. I've never forgotten the haunted look in his eyes. I've not seen or heard from him since."

How tragic, thought Marjorie.

"If you thought he was guilty then, why do you think he's innocent now?" Elsa asked.

"When I was more rational, I suspected there was more to this story because Raymond wouldn't know an original piece of art from a painted jigsaw. Numbers were his thing. He was into numbers from an early age. But then there was the evidence, which was undeniable. Raymond was the last person in the building and there was no sign of a robbery.

"It was only when I saw that man Marcus ogling your paintings, Marjorie, that I realised he had set my son up. He didn't know who I was because I've always kept my maiden name for business. I got talking to him this morning and pretended to be interested in art. The man couldn't resist bragging about his own private collection. He even offered to invite me round to look at it if I got the contract. I'm just pleased someone else got to him before I did, because if that visit had occurred and I'd seen the painting, I don't know what I'd have done."

"Surely he wouldn't openly display a stolen painting," said Elsa.

"Maybe not before, but I read recently that the real estate director died in a car crash and the company has changed hands. Because he didn't press charges, there was no crime to investigate."

"Just because a man's interested in art, it doesn't make him a thief," said Marjorie. "You said yourself that Raymond told you about the expensive art in every room at the company."

"Not before the theft; he told us afterwards. Raymond said he only learned the paintings were originals afterwards."

"And you believe Marcus set your son up and that he returned to the offices that night and stole the painting for himself?" Marjorie said.

"Yes, that's what happened." Christina appeared more sober.

"What about CCTV?" Elsa asked. "Didn't they monitor the building?"

"This all happened the week before CCTV was going to be installed by the director. Now I'm convinced that's what spurred Marcus to go ahead with his plan and take a painting."

This had given Marjorie a lot to think about. Uppermost in her mind was whether to think Christina Makepeace killed Marcus Singleton or believe what she said that someone else got there before her.

"Thank you for sharing you story, although it still doesn't prove that Marcus stole anything," said Marjorie. "I hope that someday you will heal the rift between yourself and your son. Is there anything else we can get for you?"

"No thanks, I've got a bit of a headache. I'll take some painkillers and get to sleep."

Marjorie and Elsa left Christina after Elsa had filled a large jug of water and left it at the bedside.

"If she's got a headache now, she's gonna have one hell of a headache in the morning," said Elsa.

"Indeed she is," agreed Marjorie, still deep in thought.

"Do you think she's telling the truth about not poisoning that Marcus chap?"

"If she's being honest about not knowing he would be here, then yes, but if she knew who she would be meeting on the night she arrived… well… that's another matter, and one I am going to investigate."

Chapter 16

Edna had been waiting for Horace to finish talking – or rather listening – to the rambling Bruce Melville, but she was getting impatient. She grabbed Horace's arm.

"I need to talk to you." Bruce took the hint and headed over to bend someone else's ear.

"That was rude, Edna," said Horace.

"If I'd waited for him to shut up, it would have taken all night. I'd have asked Elsa, but she's disappeared with Marge and the sozzled Christina. Why did the police change their minds about interviewing us? Did they arrest Gina?"

Horace straightened his tie before taking her arm. "I can't say anything here. Let's grab a drink and go through to Marjorie's sitting room."

"No need. There are drinks in there; you should know that by now."

"Yes, but I'm partial to mulled wine and one of those lovely young waitresses has just brought up a fresh tray."

"Lovely young waitresses! Good heavens, Horace, you are so politically incorrect."

"I don't see any harm in calling a woman lovely if she is easy on the eye, and if she happens to be working as a waitress as well… I rest my case."

"Except they're generically known as servers or waiting staff these days."

"I can't imagine that you wanted to discuss gender wars with me, Edna, as interesting as the topic might be. Do you want a glass or not?" Horace lifted two glasses of red mulled wine from the tray which was fast becoming empty. Edna snatched one from his hand, almost spilling it in the process.

"Looks like I've got one. We'd better move before anyone else grabs us." She noticed Colm McCleary heading in Horace's direction, but steered her friend out of the room before he caught up with them. They almost bumped into Fred who was shuffling along the hall.

"Where are you two going?"

"For a tête-à-tête in the sitting room. Coming?" said Horace.

Fred followed them through, looking longingly at the glasses in their hands. "Where did you get those?"

Horace opened his mouth, but Edna intervened before he started waxing lyrical about beautiful women in uniforms. "Here, have mine. I'd rather have a Scotch, anyway." She handed her glass to Fred and poured herself a whisky from Marge's drinks cabinet. "Is Marge still with that Christina woman?"

Fred flushed, making Edna wonder what had happened.

"Yes. I gave them a hand to get her upstairs, but left Marjorie and Elsa helping her get to bed. She's had a lot to drink."

"Talk about stating—"

"The bloomin' obvious," Horace finished for her, laughing loudly. "That's your catchphrase, Edna."

"Humph. I don't use it that often."

Fred opened his mouth, but closed it again, not saying anything.

"Back to the subject in hand, Horace, why did the police leave so early?" Edna sat down with her whisky in hand.

"I was wondering about that too," Fred said, plonking himself down on an armchair.

"We'll have to wait for Marjorie for the ins and outs of it, but the police left with Sally Sutherland who, for reasons unbeknown to Marjorie, appears to have fallen on her sword."

"But Sally hasn't done anything wrong," said Fred. "Why would she do that?"

"Marjorie doesn't know and didn't get the chance to ask her. Sally hasn't been arrested, but is helping police with their inquiries, as police speak goes. That's all I know."

"It makes no sense," said Edna. "I wish Elsa was here; she usually has the lowdown on what's going on. I could understand Elsa wanting to protect Marge's housekeeper, but this Sally Sutherland doesn't know any of them. They have only brought her in for this week."

"Perhaps that's where we should start," said Fred. "When I was doing my research, I didn't check her out. Or any of the other temporary staff, for that matter."

Edna was about to pooh-pooh Fred's suggestion, but saw sense. "You might be on to something there. Why was she free in the first place? It's not often cooks are short of work at the busiest time of year, is it? Fred's right; we need to do some more background checks. I wonder if Marge has references or anything."

"I doubt it. Jeremy found Sally through an agency and Marjorie didn't do the hiring," said Fred.

Horace stroked his chin. "It shouldn't be too hard to find out which agency. I could ask one of those lovely young women who are here temporarily. I suppose Jeremy recruited them from the same source, and if not, they might know where Sally came from."

"Good idea, Horace, but I'll do the asking so you don't get distracted," said Edna.

"Spoilsport," said Horace.

"I didn't check up on Gina Ratton or Elsa either – it didn't feel right," said Fred.

"Don't even think about it. Marge would be furious if you started prying into their backgrounds. Plus, I don't think there's anything to find out. Gina's worked for Marge for over thirty years and Elsa is as steady as they come."

"Should we go back in there and finish with the guests first?" Fred asked.

"Yeah, definitely. Did the talkative Bruce Melville give you any clues as to who knew what about Marcus?" Edna asked Horace.

"Nothing more than Fred told us earlier. I think he's lonely. He's the youngest here and likes to be around women. He even asked me if I'd like to go to a nightclub with him."

Edna spluttered a laugh. "Poor chap must be desperate. What did you say?"

"I said my friends would think I'd deserted them, but I told him my sons sometimes take overseas guests to Stringfellows in Leicester Square."

"I hope you told him not to bring anyone back here afterwards," said Edna.

"Not at all. I credit him with the good sense not to do such a thing. Besides, I don't think he'll go out on his own."

Edna hoped Horace's judgement was right. "He certainly didn't seem in any hurry to go while I was waiting for you to stop gabbing."

"He would need to ask Marjorie for a key and I don't think he's likely to do that under the circumstances."

"Neither should he," said Fred. "If he's here to do business, he should focus on that."

"Except the person he and the rest of them were supposed to be negotiating with went and snuffed it, didn't they?" said Edna. "And Jeremy's playing the absent host."

"I didn't like to ask Marjorie," said Horace. "I know she said he wasn't coming until tomorrow, and that he wasn't overly sorry to lose Singleton, but why do you think Jeremy isn't here?"

"Because he's most likely sucking up to this Lord and Lady someone or other. Jeremy's pretentious and his wife more so. They are what you might call socialites."

"Well, it's not right, leaving Marjorie in this predicament," said Fred.

"Be careful what you say to Marge. She and Jeremy aren't close, but she loves him and will defend him to the hilt."

"And so she should," said Horace. "My boys have their faults, but when it comes down to it, blood is blood."

Edna thought of her own brother: a gambler and a waster just like their father, but she would always back him up. Why was that?

"Speaking of families, did you hear Christina talking about her estranged son?" Horace asked.

"I think the whole bloomin' room heard. Didn't that come up in your research?" Edna fired her barb at Fred.

"Only in so much as she has a son, but I didn't think it was relevant until I heard her telling someone tonight that he had been fired from working for Marcus in the past."

"Really? That might be significant," said Horace.

"Wasn't Christina confusing Marcus with someone else?" asked Edna. "The woman was drunk and the bloke her son worked for was called Mark Singleton. I heard her saying she had never met him, she just had an old photo of him. Maybe Marcus had a brother. Anyway, you guys get back into the other room and find out where Mary Anne knew Marcus from, because she definitely did. I'll talk to one of the temps."

"Don't you mean servers?" Horace smirked.

"You're infuriating at times, Tyler."

"But you like me," Horace laughed, putting a hand on her shoulder.

"I could stay here and do an internet search on Sally," suggested Fred. "Horace is much better at socialising in these settings than I am."

Edna was about to say something, but Horace gave her a warning look.

"That would be helpful, wouldn't it, Edna?" he said.

"Yeah, very," she said, pulling a face at Horace.

The two of them left Fred with his phone.

"Right. Back into the breach," said Horace. "Wish me luck."

Edna couldn't help chuckling. Horace was a dinosaur, but an affable one who was great to have onside. If Fred was right about Sally Sutherland, it still didn't explain why she had gone to the police station, unless she was an undercover cop. No, that didn't make any sense. These were just a boring load of businesspeople with nothing to hide. Could Sally have spiked Marcus's flask, and if so, why?

It was time for Edna to do some digging of her own. She wanted the others to see how useful she could be. Sometimes she felt like she was just someone who played devil's advocate and dressed to impress in their eyes. But she had as good a brain as any of them and she was going to prove it.

Chapter 17

Edna strolled into the kitchen where three of the agency staff were finishing putting away pots and crockery from dinner.

"I don't remember signing up for this," a stroppy-looking young blonde complained while passing clean dishes from the dishwasher to a slightly older woman in her early twenties.

"We do whatever is needed and the pay's good, so I'd watch your mouth if I were you." The third woman was older still, in her forties and seemingly in charge. Her attempt to put the young woman in her place was met with an eye roll.

"Er-hum," Edna cleared her throat.

"Hello," said the older woman. "Can we get you anything?"

The young blonde rolled her eyes at her friend this time, as if Edna couldn't see her. Any other time, Edna would have given her a rollicking, but as she was after information, she chose to ignore it.

"I was looking for my friend, Lady Marjorie." A little white lie never did any harm.

"I believe she's helping one of the guests on the first floor," the young blonde woman replied while her friend sniggered, drawing a glare from their boss.

"If you've finished there, go and collect the empty glasses from the reception room."

The two young women shuffled past Edna and cackled their way along the corridor. The older woman shook her head.

"I'm sorry about them."

"We were all young once, but I can't see those two holding down a job for long. I'm Edna, by the way."

The woman sighed. "Pauline. Nice to meet you. I hate to admit it, but you're right. I'd get rid of them now if it wasn't Christmas week. They weren't expecting to work so late, but that's no excuse."

"Yeah, Marjorie was upset about losing Sally. Let's hope she'll be back tomorrow. Do you know her well?"

"No. We met for the first time yesterday. Our regular work doesn't involve a chef. Often the agency deals with everything in one package. They would usually bring in

165

outside catering and we would serve and clear away. This job's different."

"I'll say," said Edna. "Does that mean Sally's not from your agency?"

"She is on the books, but as I said, the chefs are rarely used. We were surprised she could provide cover at the busiest time of year, but she said she was using a holiday week."

"Blimey! She must have an understanding boss to give her a holiday at this time of year."

"I thought that too," said Pauline.

"Did you say Sally's a chef? Marge, I mean Marjorie, calls her a cook. Is there a difference?"

"As far as I know, the distinction is in training and place of work. A chef is qualified and works in a restaurant or a hotel, whereas a cook obviously needs some skill and basic training in food hygiene and all that, but isn't trained to the same level."

Edna liked Pauline; she was warm and friendly. All the staff wore the same purple uniforms and name badges, but without getting a lot closer, Edna wouldn't be able to make her job title out without her reading glasses.

"Interesting. Who would have thought? What's the name of the agency you work for?"

"Hungry Homes Catering and Cleaning. I don't suppose you're looking for a job?"

"Not at my age, but you never know, I might look to hire one day. Anyway, if you're going to get home tonight, I'd better stop prattling on," said Edna.

"And I'd better get on," agreed Pauline.

"Any idea where Sally works usually? We've loved her cooking, so I wouldn't mind visiting her restaurant or hotel."

"I think it's called Prince's and it's in Mayfair, but hasn't Sally been arrested?"

"Not as far as I know," said Edna, deciding it really was time to leave. "See you tomorrow."

While walking back to where she'd left Fred, Edna pondered what she'd heard. Fred was right about there being something odd with Sally's availability. Although she wasn't a Londoner herself, Edna knew Mayfair was for the rich and famous. Instead of going back into the sitting room, Edna headed upstairs to her bedroom where she called Faith.

"Hello?" A frail-sounding woman picked up the phone.

"Mum, I've told you not to answer my phone." Faith came on the line. "Hello, Edna. Sorry about that."

"Sorry to ring so late," said Edna. "I guess Horace filled you in on the death situation."

"Yes, he called earlier to say Marcus had an anaphylactic reaction... hang on a minute, Edna. Mum, you carry on with the film; I'll take this in the hall." Edna heard a door closing on the other end of the line. "Sorry, she likes to listen in on my calls and I don't want her worrying."

"No problem, but Marcus was poisoned," said Edna. She heard a gasp.

"What is it with you four and murder?"

"You're the one who called us the awesome foursome in the first place."

Faith chuckled. "I'm going to change it to the fatal four."

"Don't you dare!"

"Okay, we'll stick to the awesome foursome, but fatal four also fits. Are you ringing to cancel tomorrow?"

"No. As far as I'm aware, the outing's still on. I wanted to ask you if you knew anything about a restaurant in Mayfair called Prince's."

"I do. It's where the rich and powerful go. The likes of pop stars, royalty and other famous people have eaten there. Are you thinking of taking Marjorie's houseguests?"

"I don't think so, but I could ask Marge," Edna chortled loudly. She was about to explain why she wanted to know, but heard Faith's mother calling for her. "Look, I'll let you get back to your film and see you in the morning."

Edna typed into her phone and looked up the number of Prince's. The telephone was answered immediately by someone sounding as plummy as Marge.

"Good evening. This is Prince's Fine Dining. How may I help you?"

"I was hoping to speak to Sally Sutherland, if she's not too busy."

"Our chefs are always busy, madam, but I'm afraid I can't help you. Ms Sutherland is not in this week."

"Oh, do you know when she'll be back from her holiday?" Edna pressed.

"Ms Sutherland is off sick this week, not on holiday." The woman hesitated, maybe fearing she had said too much. "Who shall I say called?"

"Sorry to hear she's sick. I'll give her a ring at home," Edna said before pressing the call end button. Intrigued and puzzled, Edna debated her next move. Why would Sally call in sick from her day job to take a week's agency work? She was either desperate for money, or up to no good.

"I'll show Marge I can investigate too," she said to the air before leaving the room. Edna checked the landing was clear before she made her way to the stairs at the far end, which led to the second floor. As far as she knew, all Jeremy's guests were staying on the first. Horace and Frederick were on the second, but they were downstairs right now, and the only other person who had been given one of the four rooms up there was Sally.

Edna opened the first door she came to and recognised Horace's suitcase. She resisted the temptation to have a mooch around and closed it again. It was when she entered the room at the far end that she knew she was in the right place. The potent smell of dog greeted her.

Edna didn't know why she was tiptoeing, but it might have had something to do with the guilt of being in somebody else's bedroom. She thought back to when she and Fred had checked out a dead man's room during their Highland holiday and grinned.

At first glance, she noted that Sally was exceptionally neat and tidy, despite the dog odour which made Edna want to open a window. The bedside table would be the best place to start, so Edna sat on the edge of the bed, which creaked under her load.

"All right, all right. I'll start dieting in the New Year," she said as if the bed had complained. There was a novel with a bookmark on top of the table, which she ignored, instead opening the first drawer. Inside, she found a phone charger, a travel jewellery box containing a necklace and what looked like an antique ring. There was also a wristwatch. Edna leaned down and opened the door to the cupboard, which was disappointingly sparse, containing just a few more books. Sally clearly enjoyed reading.

Edna got up off the bed to another disapproving creak, sounding almost like a groan. "You're lucky I'm not sleeping in here. I'd give you what for," she said before giving her right cheek a few light slaps. "Edna! You're talking to a bloomin' mattress."

There didn't seem to be anything else in the room, but she checked the wardrobe and pulled out the empty suitcase, opening it up to see whether there were any clues inside. There was nothing.

"Blimey! Your life is more boring than mine, Sally Sutherland," she said. Taking another look around the room, she opened the drawers in the chest next to the wardrobe, but there was no hidden poison lurking in the chef's underwear.

Edna sighed heavily. "What did you expect to find?"

"A confession would have been handy," she replied to herself, giggling.

A sudden tiredness came over her. These episodes of exhaustion were a hangover from the cancer treatment she'd had and could take her by surprise. Sometimes she would fall asleep at her dining-room table for no reason. The doctors had told her not to worry about it, but they weren't the ones who had been treated for cancer.

Edna removed her shoes and sat on the bed again. The creak was even louder when she put her feet up.

"Look, bed, I just need a couple of minutes, then I'll be on my way, so stop your moaning." Despite its age and its groaning, the mattress was surprisingly comfortable. Edna sat for a few moments, trying to get the measure of Sally Sutherland from the room, but nothing came to her.

Seeing the book to her left, she picked it up. It was a Maureen Lee novel. As she flicked through the pages, a black-and-white photo of a couple of teenagers dropped out.

Suddenly, she recalled the contents of the bedside cupboard. Swinging her legs back over the side of the bed to an even louder groan, she opened the door again and took out the dog-eared book on top of the pile. *The Adoptee's Guide to DNA Testing: How to Use Genetic Genealogy to Discover Your Long-Lost Family.* Edna opened the pages and leafed through the documents inside.

"So that's what this is all about."

Edna put the book back and hurried along the second-floor landing, down the first flight of stairs with a sense of urgency and excitement. Her breathing wouldn't allow her to hurry any more, so she took the wider staircase to the ground floor at a more measured pace. She saw the light shining from under the door of Marge's study. She knocked and pushed open the door.

"You'll never believe what I—" Edna felt a freezing cold chill and saw that the window was wide open. "Some people were born in a barn." She stomped towards the window, but didn't get there. Someone shoved her over. A sharp pain shot through her and she fell to the ground.

Dazed, but not unconscious, she heard a key turn in the lock from the outside. She tried to sit up, but the pain in her left shoulder was excruciating, so she lowered her head down onto the rug.

"It's s-s-soooo c-c-c-cold," she said before everything went black.

Chapter 18

Elsa assured Marjorie she would come in early in the morning and that she and Gina could handle the breakfasts if Sally wasn't back by then. Marjorie asked Elsa to check on Hercules and make sure he wasn't pining too much before she left.

Her thoughts turned once more to why Sally hadn't told the police that Gina had prepared Marcus's lunch. "Unless, of course, Gina didn't prepare the flask. That would explain it." Marjorie spoke out loud. What it didn't explain was what plausible motive Sally could have for poisoning the unpleasant man, but it made more sense than Marjorie's long-term friend and housekeeper having anything to do with the matter.

The sound of chattering came from her reception room. Marjorie took a deep breath in, hoping the guests would go to bed soon. Edna and her other friends were nowhere to be seen. Looking around at Jeremy's guests, she felt unusually vulnerable. Was there a killer among them? One of the agency staff was filling a tray with empty glasses, ready to clear away.

"Ah, Lady Marjorie, we were just wondering when Jeremy might join us." Bruce and Elmur's faces were flushed from drinking what looked like mulled wine from the remnants in the glasses they were holding.

"Didn't I say earlier? He has business all day tomorrow, but will be here for dinner in the evening."

"I would have preferred to get on with things," Elmur murmured loud enough for Marjorie to hear, but he wasn't looking at her.

"I realise you would have been in meetings with Marcus this evening, gentlemen, but these are exceptional circumstances beyond our control. Besides, tomorrow is already arranged with plans you were enthusiastic about, if I remember." Marjorie felt tired and irritable, but her irritation was more with her son for leaving her in this position than with anything Elmur had said. She couldn't understand why they wanted to go ahead with their outing, either.

"That was before we knew a man was poisoned. I'm not sure I want to stay in a house where cooks go around poisoning people."

"I can assure you, Mr Cartwright, none of my staff had anything to do with the death of Marcus Singleton. But you are free to avail yourself of a hotel if you wish. I expect the police would prefer you to stay in the locality, though, until they sort everything out."

"There's no need for that. Anyway, it's late."

"Indeed," said Marjorie.

"If the cook didn't poison him, who did?" Bruce asked.

"That's for the police to find out. I'm sure they'll find the person responsible soon enough," Marjorie said with more certainty than she felt.

"We heard the cook was arrested." Elmur wasn't to be put off so easily, it seemed.

"I don't know where you got that information from, but it's not true."

Marjorie followed Elmur's glance towards the slender woman in her early twenties with bright red hair, who was leaving the room with a full tray. At least that told her who had spread the gossip.

"We should wait and see what happens, Elmur. It could still turn out to be accidental poisoning, you know. These things happen. It only takes someone to put the wrong thing in the wrong place, and let's face it, Marjorie's cook would have no reason to kill Singleton, would she? Whereas a few people in this room might have – you included." Bruce's statement was innocent enough, but it had a profound effect on Elmur, whose face turned purple, then pale.

"I'm going to bed," he snapped. "Goodnight, Lady Marjorie." Elmur forced the words out before scurrying towards the door. Marjorie stared after him. She had thought him a pleasant man, even after discovering he had a weakness for gambling the currency markets.

"Don't mind him, Lady Marjorie. He's stressed out."

"Frederick mentioned his gambling," said Marjorie. "Perhaps he lost a lot of money today and that's what's bothering him."

Bruce thought for a moment before answering. "It could be that; he was in a bad mood when he got back from the market earlier. But I reckon he's got family troubles. His wife phoned him a while ago and I got the impression she wasn't too happy about something."

Marjorie nodded, understanding. "I expect she would like him home."

"Or not," said Bruce. "I heard him telling Colm the marriage is on the rocks, and when I spoke to Colm later, he reckoned it was down to his gambling."

Marjorie wondered at how easy it was to glean information about people's private lives. Bruce obviously had nothing better to do than to gossip.

"Are you married, Mr Melville?"

"No. I wouldn't want to settle down. I've got a girlfriend in Budapest. She owns an art gallery over there. Viki, her name is. She'd like to settle down, but I prefer things the way they are."

Marjorie suspected Bruce Melville and his charming ways wouldn't be lost on women and that he preferred the best of both worlds.

"And do you like art yourself?"

"Not a bit. While I can appreciate a good painting, I prefer sport. I play a lot of golf and tennis, and when I'm not doing those things, I'm at the gym. I'm also a fan of nightclubs. Your friend Horace mentioned Stringfellows was a good place to go."

"If Horace says so, it most probably is, but I wouldn't know. Why don't you ask Faith in the morning? She knows everything about London and most other places."

"Thank you, I will," he said. Marjorie got the impression he wanted to say something else, but she was rescued when Horace joined them.

"I'll say goodnight then," said Bruce. Colm and Melissa followed him out, the latter giving Marjorie and Horace a wave.

"Where were you?" Marjorie asked.

"In your sitting room having a conflab," said Horace.

Mary Anne placed an empty glass on one of the serving trolleys and called over, "Did Christina get to bed okay?"

"Yes, she did. I expect she'll suffer for it in the morning, though," said Marjorie.

Mary Anne grinned. "Let's hope she has a lapse of memory as well or she'll be so embarrassed. Anyway, it's getting late; I'm going to head on up myself. Thank you for hosting us, Marjorie. It can't be easy at this time of year having a house full of strangers. I hope Sally is back tomorrow; she's a wonderful cook."

With the parting shot out of the way, Mary Anne followed the others just as Elsa came in.

"All gone, I see," she said.

"Just," said Marjorie. "And so should you be. Would you like Johnson to give you a lift home?"

"No, I'll walk. It's not far."

"I won't hear of you walking alone at this time of night," said Horace. "I'll walk you." He hustled Elsa from the room, not standing for any argument. "And then I'll ask Marjorie how Mary Anne knew the police had gone off with the cook."

Elsa laughed. "I can tell you that. We have a chatterbox temp among us. See you in the morning, Marjorie."

Marjorie mouthed a thank you to Horace before going into the sitting room for a nightcap. Frederick was hunched over his tablet.

"Hello, Marjorie, I take it she's down?"

"I sincerely hope so," said Marjorie. "Would you like a brandy?"

"Yes, please."

"It seems everyone knows about Sally going to the police station." She handed him a drink and sat down with one of her own.

"How?" asked Frederick. "Edna and I have not long found out. That's why we met in here, away from listening ears."

"It appears we have a talkative waitress. The one with flame-red hair, so be careful what you say around her," said Marjorie. "Which reminds me: I'd better thank the temporary staff for staying on so late. If you're staying up, I'll finish my nightcap with you when I get back."

"I'll wait to drink mine then and finish with this," said Frederick, turning his attention back to the tablet. Without asking him what he was doing, she left the room.

Marjorie heard the front door close again while she was walking towards the kitchen. The agency staff had made light work of the washing up, and the dishwasher was running. There was no sign of them, so she assumed they'd made haste to leave once they were done. She could thank them in the morning.

A gust of air gave her a chill. "Someone's left the back door open. I hope they haven't let Hercules run off."

Marjorie heard scratching, then barking and growling coming from the scullery. She opened the door and Hercules shot past her, through the back door. Elsa must have forgotten to put him out before she left.

Marjorie braved the ice-cold air and turned on the patio light, but there was no sign of the big beast. She heard barking in the distance. Shivering with cold, she grabbed an old overcoat from a hook, pulled on a pair of Wellington boots that were far too big for her and stepped warily onto the frosty patio. The dog sounded like a demented wolf in the distance.

"Oh, do come on, Hercules. I can't stand here all night," she called. There was no sign of him, but the barking continued. Marjorie took the steps down onto the frozen lawn, her teeth chattering as she walked towards the barking. "Your owner has a lot to answer for," she muttered before calling loudly. "Hercules. Come!"

The barking stopped briefly, then resumed. There was nothing for it but to find the blasted dog. Sally had given her the responsibility of taking care of him.

The noise sounded like it was coming from the west wall. Marjorie trod carefully through the trees and shrubs, finding the path more by luck than design. The ice-cold air stung her cheeks. She wouldn't normally venture out here in the dark, and certainly not without a torch.

"Hercules!" Marjorie called again, wondering if she should go back for a torch.

Loud rustling grabbed her attention and Hercules emerged from the laurel nearby. Her hand flew to her chest.

"You gave me a fright. Now, come on back to the house."

The dog turned back, and she lost sight of him again. She heard more barking, but it was much closer this time. Cursing herself for not thinking of bringing a lead, she took tentative steps into the bushes where leaves scrunched beneath her feet. She was almost at the wall when she saw Hercules's shadow. He had stopped barking.

"Look, Hercules. I'm sorry Sally isn't here, but this behaviour is just not acceptable. Now come along before—"

Marjorie stopped suddenly. Her new charge was standing over someone lying in a heap of leaves. Had the dog caught a burglar? She heard groaning and stepped in closer to where the moonlight revealed a woman lying on the ground.

"What on earth are you doing out here?"

Chapter 19

Christina Makepeace appeared dazed. Her wild eyes blinked at Marjorie, who was pleased the cloud had moved and moonlight was giving her a clear view of the scene.

"Can you stand?" Marjorie asked.

Christina moved into a sitting position and tried to stand, but when she put her left foot to the ground, she squealed.

Hercules growled. "Move out of the way, you big brute," Marjorie said, patting Hercules on the head.

"I must have twisted my ankle. Whose is that dog?"

"He belongs to Sally, the cook. I'm not sure what happened to you, but we can discuss that once you're inside the house. Try to keep warm and stay here…" it was rather a stupid thing to say under the circumstances, "…I'll get help." Hercules moved back to his guarding position.

"Good boy, Hercules. You stay too. If you get too cold, Christina, you can always snuggle up to him."

Christina looked at the dog doubtfully.

Obeying Marjorie's command, Hercules sat down with his enormous tongue hanging out of his mouth. In the moonlight, the garden looked like a scene from a cinematic poster, except for the presence of the dishevelled woman sitting up in the stack of leaves. Marjorie walked as fast as she could with the absence of her walking stick, arriving back at the house. She found Horace and Frederick in her sitting room next to the glowing fire.

"There you are. I hope you don't mind; I just added some logs to the fire—" Horace stopped speaking when he took in her condition. "What's happened?"

"It's Christina. She's had a fall in the garden and can't walk. She seems to have twisted an ankle. I've left Hercules with her, but she needs help."

"Come along, Fred. Damsel in distress." Horace was up in an instant.

"Shouldn't we call the other men? They're much younger than us," said Frederick. Marjorie couldn't work out whether he was generally unfit or not wanting a repeat of his earlier encounter with Christina in her bedroom.

"There's no time for that. By the time they get dressed, the poor woman will be a block of ice. Besides, I'm as fit as I've ever been, but if you're not up to it…" Horace let his words hang, leaving Frederick to ponder the challenge.

It didn't take him long to agree, albeit with some reluctance. "I'll help, but I'm getting my hat and coat. You can go out there in your shirt if you want to."

"Agreed," said Horace. "What's the ground like underfoot, Marjorie?" Horace's enthusiasm appeared to be wavering on examination of his shiny polished black shoes.

"It's frosty, so not too much mud. There are boots on the boot rack used by the gardener and his assistant. They might fit."

Once the men had hurriedly put coats on, Marjorie went with them as far as the back door, where Horace changed into the gardener's boots. Frederick kept his own shoes on.

"Ready," said Horace.

Marjorie pointed in the direction of the far right-hand corner of the garden. "Take the steps down from the patio and head diagonally right. You'll find her at the back with Hercules keeping guard. Do you think I should call a doctor?"

"Let's wait and see what the damage is, shall we?" said Horace. "By the way, have you seen Edna on your travels? She went to have a word with some of your agency staff and didn't come back. Elsa said she hadn't seen her, but she hadn't gone back to the kitchen. One of the temps was annoying her, so she left them to it."

"Oh dear. I didn't see Edna just now, but she might have gone to bed."

Creases lined Horace's forehead. "She's most likely still nattering to one of them somewhere. First things first. Come on, Fred."

"It's Frederick," Marjorie heard Frederick mutter, then, "With the time it's taken us to get ready, we could have called the others to help."

"You might be right, but we're here now."

The voices trailed off in the distance and Marjorie went back inside. She hadn't wanted to worry Horace by telling him the agency staff had already gone home when he had other things on his mind. It wasn't unusual for Edna to get sidetracked. The priority right now was getting Christina Makepeace back inside.

Marjorie put the kettle on and, against her better judgement, added tea bags to a pot. Gloria had persuaded her to buy some for simplicity's sake. No doubt Christina would need a hot drink when she came in. Marjorie shuddered to imagine what might have happened to her had Hercules not found her.

"Silly woman, why couldn't she just sleep the alcohol off like anyone else would have done?" Marjorie placed mugs on the kitchen table, sighing. People seemed to prefer mugs to teacups these days. The large range kept the kitchen warm and toasty, even though the door was open. She often sat in front of it when sleep eluded her.

Hercules bounded into the kitchen, looking very pleased with himself. "And so you should," Marjorie said. "Good boy. I wonder what Sally gives you for treats." Marjorie opened the larder fridge and found a tub of cooked sausages. "One of these will do nicely."

She took a sausage and held it out, hoping Sally had taught the dog not to snatch or she might lose a finger. For such a large dog, he took the sausage with amazing gentleness, his teeth coming nowhere near her. Marjorie patted him on the head.

"I'm pleased to see you have manners befitting the aristocracy."

Hercules swallowed the sausage in one go.

"Hmm. A work in progress, perhaps."

Horace and Frederick's arrival was heralded by puffing and panting from Frederick and groaning from Christina, who hobbled in with one arm around each of the men's shoulders. They supported her into a chair.

The kettle whistled on the range.

"I haven't heard that sound for many a year," said Horace.

"We use an electric kettle or a water heater most of the time, but I always use the old one when I'm here on my own. Force of habit, I suppose." Marjorie's thoughts wandered into the distant past when she and Ralph would enjoy a late-night drink by themselves.

"You sit down, Marjorie, I'll get tea." Frederick filled the teapot, pleased to be released from Christina, no doubt. He was still out of puff and his forehead was clammy when he removed his hat, whereas Horace had barely broken a sweat.

Horace took another chair and pulled off the gardener's boots, swapping them for his shoes. Marjorie tried not to look at the mud and leaves trailing through the kitchen.

"Any sign of Edna?" Horace asked.

Marjorie shook her head. "I haven't looked yet. I'll check her room in a little while. Now, my dear—" Marjorie got up again and went into the scullery, returning with a woollen shawl she had inherited from her mother. She wrapped it around Christina's shoulders before sitting down again. "How's the ankle?"

With mugs of hot tea in front of them, the three friends and Hercules watched Christina, waiting for answers. Christina manoeuvred herself into a position where she could shift her ankle beneath the table.

"It's not too bad. I might have sprained it, but it's feeling better already. If it's swollen in the morning, I'll get it checked out. I assume you have a doctor nearby?"

"There's a walk-in centre not too far away for minor injuries. We could take you tonight, if you wish?" Marjorie's offer was halfhearted and the 'we' meant Horace and a taxi. She wouldn't want to call Johnson out this late at night.

"I don't think there's any need tonight." Christina helped herself to two spoonfuls of sugar and drank greedily from her mug, draining it quickly. Frederick topped it up for her.

"Why on earth did you go for a walk in the dark?" Horace asked.

"I didn't… well, not exactly. I came down for a cigarette. It's one of my secret pleasures, but when I heard noises in the hall, I made my way to the kitchen. There was nobody in the kitchen, but the back door was open, so I went outside. There was a sound coming from the side of the house and I went to see if it was one of the others. The next thing I know is this big lump," she looked at Hercules, "was standing over me, barking his head off. I thought he was going to eat me, but then Marjorie came along."

"Do you remember tripping over?" Frederick asked.

Christina shook her head. "No. I think I felt something like pressure on my neck and I must have passed out. The drink might have caught up with me, I suppose."

"That doesn't explain how you ended up in the southwest corner of my garden," said Marjorie.

"Is that where I was?" Christina slurped back the second mug of tea, shaking her head. "I really can't help unless I was sleepwalking. Right now, I've had enough excitement for one day. If you'll excuse me, I think I'll go to bed." Christina stood, making an unenthusiastic attempt at putting weight on her ankle. "Would you mind?" She looked at Horace.

"Not at all," he said, putting his arm around her waist. "Hang on to me."

When the two of them left the kitchen, Hercules released a guttural growl.

"Now, now. There's no need for jealousy. I know you rescued her, but a sausage was your reward. Now, did you do your business while you were outside?"

Hercules's big round eyes gazed adoringly into Marjorie's.

"If I didn't know better, I'd say he's flirting with you," said Frederick, laughing. "Be careful, Marjorie, or you might find yourself owning the heavy lump."

"Not on your life." She turned to Hercules again. "Do you need to go outside?"

The dog jumped up and walked back into the annexe towards the back door.

"It seems that's a yes. I'll let him out." said Frederick. "He's a big softie when you get to know him, isn't he?"

So long as you're not an alpha male, thought Marjorie, but said, "I'm just pleased he found Christina. If she'd been out there much longer, she might have got hypothermia. It's going to be sub-zero later."

"I'd say it already is," said Frederick.

"After he's been outside, would you mind putting him in the scullery and making sure he has a bowl of water? Sally made a bed for him in there and he's not sleeping in my room. I'd better see if I can find Edna. She'll be fast asleep in her bed, no doubt."

Marjorie felt exhaustion creeping in. What a day it had been. All she needed to do now was check Edna was tucked up in bed and get some sleep herself. Tomorrow couldn't be as bad as today, surely?

Chapter 20

Marjorie knocked lightly on Edna's door. When there was no reply, she opened it slightly. The hinges squeaked, reminding her to ask Elsa or Gina to oil them. Pushing the door open forty-five degrees allowed enough light to enter without waking anyone asleep, but the caution was not required. The room was empty.

Marjorie flicked the light switch and called from outside the en suite, "Edna? Are you in there?" Again, there was no reply. Marjorie checked inside, hoping her cousin-in-law hadn't fallen, but it was empty and everywhere was dry. Edna had not been in the bathroom recently.

She reentered the bedroom and found Horace poking his head around the door, eyes questioning. Marjorie shook her head.

"She's not here. Perhaps we should phone her."

Horace nodded, removing his phone from a trouser pocket. A ringtone blared from the bed. Marjorie saw Edna's mobile phone glowing and jumping around near the pillow.

"Blast," said Horace. "Now I'm seriously worried. She never goes anywhere without her phone." He crossed the room and picked it up.

"What are you doing?" Marjorie asked, seeing Horace swiping and tapping.

"After that carry on in Romania, she gave me her passcode. I'm just checking whether she's made any calls that might tell us where she is."

"And has she?"

"She made two about an hour ago. One to an unknown number and one to Faith. I'll try the unknown first." Horace pressed the redial, but was quick to say, "Sorry. Wrong number." He looked at her. "That was Prince's in Mayfair."

"I know the place. Ralph and I used to dine there, but that was a long time ago. Very chic and expensive, as I recall."

"Yes, I've taken important clients in the past. Why would Edna be ringing them? I'll see if Faith knows anything about it." Before Marjorie could protest that it was far too late to be calling anyone, Horace had pressed dial, this time using his own phone.

"Faith, I'm sorry to call so late, but is Edna with you?" Horace listened intently for a few minutes with the occasional question, and then rang off. "She called Faith to ask her about Prince's, but didn't say why. Do you think she's gone to the restaurant?" Horace's eyes were wide with worry.

"No, and certainly not without that contraption. She must be in the house somewhere. We'll find Frederick and search the ground floor. We can also check her coat is still in the hall. Don't worry, Horace, we'll find her. What did you say she was doing again?"

"Asking the temporary staff which agency they and hopefully Sally worked for."

"Well, they're long gone. Why did you want to know about the agency?"

"Fred had an idea that there was more to the cook, Sally, being here. He couldn't understand why she would be free to take up this job the week before Christmas. We also wanted to know why the police were interested enough in her to take her to the station."

"I see," said Marjorie. "When you put it like that, it does seem strange. I was hoping to ask Sally about the latter tomorrow; the police don't have enough evidence to charge her, so I'm sure they will let her go. That is, if she doesn't do anything silly."

"Like what?" Horace asked as they reached the ground floor.

"I don't know exactly. For some reason, she's protecting Gina, one of the agency workers or myself. She can't have a motive for killing Marcus, so cannot be responsible for his poisoning. Still, that's a conversation for later. Right now, we need to find Edna."

Looking over at the coatrack, Marjorie saw Edna's coat, hat and scarf hanging there. She was definitely somewhere in the house, then, although after what had happened to Christina, Marjorie wouldn't take anything for granted. She was feeling lightheaded and her heart was pounding in her chest. Only then did she realise how much she had come to care for her cousin-in-law.

Frederick was pacing the sitting room when they found him. "Well? Has that woman gone to bed and is Edna asleep?"

"Yes, Christina should be tucked up now, but we haven't found Edna," said Horace. "Her outdoor things are still hanging in the hall, though."

"She can't have gone far then. Get her scarf. I know who can help," said Frederick.

Horace did as he was asked. He gave the scarf to Frederick, who marched off towards the kitchen.

"I think I know what he has in mind," said Marjorie, opening the library and checking it was empty.

"I wonder if she found out something from the agency staff and is checking Sally's room," Horace said.

Before Marjorie had the chance to say how sensible his suggestion was, Hercules appeared, tail wagging furiously, with Frederick panting behind. "He hasn't even sniffed it yet. He ran off as soon as I opened the door."

Hercules stopped to allow a brief pat on the head before bounding up the stairs. Marjorie sighed.

"At least we know where he's heading. Horace just suggested that Edna might be in Sally's room, so perhaps we should all go upstairs."

"You wait here, Marjorie. We'll go. I'll be back down as soon as we've found her," Horace said.

"We'd better get on with it before that dog wakes up the entire household. It's a good job we're the only ones on the second floor, Horace," said Frederick.

"Thank you both. I'll wait here, but Frederick's right, you'd better hurry." Marjorie stood at the foot of the stairs for a few moments listening, worried Hercules might start barking, but all was quiet. The hall light switched itself off. It was on a motion sensor timer at Jeremy's insistence because he worried if she tried to turn lights off whilst carrying a tray up to her room, she might fall. They had argued about it, but acknowledging Jeremy's worries were rational, she had agreed.

It was then she noticed a light coming from under her study door. She walked to the door and found it locked.

"Hello? Hello? Who's in there? Edna? Is it you?"

She heard a groan. "Marjorie, help me." Edna's voice sounded frail and weak.

Edna's use of her full name sent shivers down Marjorie's spine. Her cousin-in-law must be in real trouble. "I'm coming, Edna." With her heart feeling as if it would explode in her chest, she checked the lock. The key wasn't inside. "Can you unlock the door?" Marjorie called.

"I… I don't have a key. S-s-someone l-l-locked it."

Horace, Frederick and Hercules had appeared behind Marjorie as she turned, knees and legs trembling. "She's locked in there. I think she's hurt."

"Stand aside, I'll break it down," said Horace, taking steps back to barge through the door.

Despite her anxious state, Marjorie held her ground. "It will be much quicker and far less damaging with a key. There's a bunch of keys in the cabinet beside the front door."

Horace stared at the solid oak door, perhaps realising who would have come off worse from that particular battle, and then flew to the front door. He was back in seconds.

"Which one?"

Marjorie took the keys, but found her hands too shaky to hold them. They dropped to the floor. Frederick was the calmest one among them. He picked the keys up and, after donning reading glasses, checked each label. Horace and Hercules were panting and huffing like engines raring to go, and Marjorie felt as though she might faint. All was silent behind the door.

"Hurry up, man," said Horace.

Hercules whined in agreement.

"I'm going as fast as I can." Frederick finally found the right key and put it in the lock. It was stiff and took a few attempts before turning. He opened the door into the ice-cold room.

Horace pushed past and was on his knees next to Edna in moments. Tears threatened to fall from Marjorie's eyes when the first thing he did was replace the wig that was lying close by her head.

"It's all right, old girl. We're here. Are you hurt?"

Edna's teeth chattered so loudly she could hardly speak. Frederick had the presence of mind to close the window and phone for an ambulance.

"We need to get her warm," said Horace.

As if knowing what was required, Hercules lay down behind Edna, snuggling into her back while Frederick fetched coats from the hall.

"S-s-s-s-sorry, I, I, I don't think I'm going to make it," Edna said, bottom lip trembling along with the rest of her.

Marjorie's heart swelled with sorrow at seeing her powerful cousin lying there, as white as a ghost. Edna's left upper arm looked displaced. She fought back tears.

"Now you listen to me, Edna Parkinton. You hang on in there. Help is on the way."

"N-n-not s-s-sure I can," Edna said.

Horace rubbed her good hand while Frederick went to stand at the front door and wait for the ambulance.

"Don't talk like that, Edna. Just rest for now."

A single paramedic appeared as Marjorie found herself welling up for the second time. After asking them a few questions, the paramedic learned the only thing Marjorie and company knew about the incident was the patient's name and age. Her assessment included checking Edna's vital signs. Afterwards, she spoke into her radio using words like hypothermia, thready pulse and possible fractured clavicle. She requested a red ambulance, which Marjorie assumed meant urgent.

While they waited for the ambulance, the paramedic removed a silver blanket from her bag and, with Horace's help, wrapped it around Edna. Horace helped Edna to sit up while avoiding touching the left arm. Two more paramedics in greens arrived minutes later and one of them, a large man, asked the same questions again while a rake-thin woman helped the first responder to stabilise the injured shoulder. At one point, Edna cried out. Marjorie saw Horace cringe as if he were the one suffering pain.

The large man tried again. "Did any of you witness the fall?"

Edna yelled. "No!"

"It's okay, Edna." Horace tried to calm her, assuming she was in pain.

Edna's colour was returning to her face, as was her bluntness. "Not that, idiot. I didn't fall. I was pushed."

"Are you sure, Mrs Parkinton? You had a very low temperature, which can cause confusion," the male paramedic said.

"I know the difference between a fall and a push, and I ain't five years old, so don't talk to me like I am. And I'm not senile either."

Marjorie would normally feel embarrassed by Edna's outburst, but this one made her heart leap.

"She's going to be just fine," said Frederick, grinning. He had been standing in the doorway, allowing the others to get on with their work.

"And what the hell's that smell?" Edna yelled.

"Hercules has been keeping you warm while we waited for the experts," explained Horace.

"Well, thanks, Hercules, but you're dismissed. That dog could really do with a bath, not to mention breath freshener. And you could do with finding someone to do your ironing, mate." Edna spoke those words to the large paramedic. The woman who was with him grinned.

"I've been telling him that for years. Come on, Mrs Parkinton, let's get you to the hospital."

"I ain't going to no hospital. They're full of germs."

Marjorie felt it was time to intervene. "Edna Parkinton, unless you want your arm to set in that position, you will jolly well do as you're told for once in your life."

The large paramedic had made a hasty retreat and reappeared with a stretcher trolley, which he lowered to the floor.

"All right, Marge, but I'm not staying."

"We can discuss that later," said Marjorie, feeling almost relieved to hear Edna use the diminutive of her name again. The three professionals assisted Edna onto the trolley and strapped her in before raising it high.

"Will you be accompanying us?" The man looked hopefully towards Marjorie.

"Lady Marjorie's got guests staying. I'll come, if I may," said Horace, winking at Edna. "I'll make sure she doesn't give you any trouble."

"Are you her husband, sir?" the man asked. They all waited for a second outburst from Edna, but she just sat back against the pillows on the trolley, grinning.

"He should be so lucky," she said.

"Just a good friend. I'm Horace Tyler. This is Marjorie Snellthorpe, Edna's cousin."

Edna looked questioningly in Marjorie's direction, clearly expecting her to correct it to cousin-in-law, but Marjorie didn't say anything.

"And that's Fred Mackworth."

"Frederick," said Frederick, rolling his eyes.

"Right. We'd best be on our way. Would you mind following us in your car, sir?" the large paramedic said to Horace.

"Can't he come with me?" Edna looked at the man. "Please, I'll be on my best behaviour."

Marjorie giggled. "Don't believe her."

The ambulance crew and first responder laughed and the woman in greens said, "Sure he can. Come on, Mr Tyler."

"Call me Horace, please."

"You're not coming if you're going to start with your flirting, Horace Tyler."

Marjorie gave Horace a front door key before he left, then she and Frederick stood at the door, watching Edna being loaded into the ambulance. Horace took the seat opposite her once he was allowed inside and held her hand. The thin paramedic, who was travelling in the back, closed the doors, and the large man drove away. Then the first responder came back to speak to Marjorie.

"Do you believe someone pushed your cousin over?"

"I think they may have," said Marjorie.

"Would it have been by mistake? The dog, perhaps?"

"I fear not," she said. "Hercules was with us."

"Could your cousin be confused?"

"If the door hadn't been locked from the outside, I'd say possibly."

"In which case, I'll need to inform the police. They should be able to interview her at the hospital. I'll ask them not to disturb you again tonight. You both look done in."

"Where will Edna be taken?" Marjorie asked.

"Most likely the Royal Free Hospital. You go to bed now. You've had a terrible shock. Good job you found her. It was touch and go there for a bit."

Chapter 21

Having slept fitfully, Marjorie rose early and made her way to the kitchen to make herself a cup of tea. Horace's head jerked upwards when she walked in. Hercules responded to her entry with a low whine and an apathetic tail wag, but remained recumbent at Horace's feet.

"I'm sorry to wake you, but I wanted an early morning cuppa before the mayhem begins. I see you two have bonded."

"I wasn't asleep," said Horace, rubbing his eyes. "Hercules and I have been discussing the events of last night."

"Mm," said Marjorie. "What time did you get back? And how was the patient when you left her?"

"The patient is upstairs in bed. We got a taxi back here at about four in the morning. I was past sleeping by that time, so Hercules and I have been keeping each other company. He's pining over his owner.

"The doctor fixed Edna's arm. The shoulder was dislocated, not broken. She has to wear a sling and doesn't need to be seen again until she returns home. They'll refer her for a follow up in the New Year."

"At least we have some good news, then. Will she need help washing and dressing?"

"Definitely for the top half or she could end up doing herself more damage." Horace grinned. "You should have heard her giving the consultant what for when he manipulated the shoulder in A&E."

"I can imagine. Didn't she need an anaesthetic?"

"No. Once he had the X-ray results, he did it there and then, after giving her painkillers and a sedative."

"I remember someone having that procedure performed following nitrous oxide, better known as laughing gas," said Marjorie.

"Edna could have done with some of that because she certainly wasn't laughing."

Marjorie prepared tea in a pot, chuckling. "I get the picture. But on a more serious note, did she see who it was she says pushed her?"

"No. She said she was looking for you and saw the light on in your study. She knocked and went in. When she realised the window was open, she went to close it. That's when someone – who must have been hiding behind the door—"

"Having heard her knock," said Marjorie.

"Precisely. That's when they pushed past her and locked her in. I doubt they meant to cause her any actual harm. More likely they wanted to avoid being seen, but I'd still like to get my hands on them. She said she put her arm out and felt something go. It was the shock of it made her pass out and the cold kept her down."

Marjorie placed the pot of tea on the table and poured for them both. "Now all we need to know is what this person was doing in my study," she said.

Horace reached under the table and pulled a briefcase out, placing it on the top. "Trying to take this. After Edna went to bed, I checked the study and found it on the ground just outside the window. I reckon whoever barged into Edna was about to follow it when she knocked."

"So why didn't they collect it after knocking her over?"

"My guess is, they didn't know they'd caused her damage and thought she would have picked it up when she saw the window open."

"Either that or they were frightened of being seen," said Marjorie.

Horace drained the mug Marjorie had given him while she sipped tea from a cup. She sat back thoughtfully.

"Did you find anything in the briefcase?"

"It's locked. I thought we should tell the police this is what the intruder, or guest, was looking for. They came to the hospital. Did you call them?"

"It was the first responder. She said she would call them when I told her we found Edna locked inside the room. Was it Inspector Crow?"

"No. It was two uniformed officers. They didn't seem that interested, and Edna wasn't in the mood to answer questions."

"I don't expect they connected it to the murder at a Christmas market. Why would they?" Marjorie said.

At that moment, Frederick arrived. "Is it okay if I join you?"

"Of course," said Marjorie. "Have some tea while Horace brings you up to date."

"At least she's going to be all right. I was worried there for a bit," said Frederick after Horace had filled him in on the hospital visit, the diagnosis, treatment, the police visit and the briefcase.

"Me too," said Horace, staring into space.

"What had Edna been doing before she got to the study?" Marjorie asked.

Horace suddenly perked up, slapping his forehead. "Of course. Sorry, you don't know, do you? My head's not functioning properly this morning. Edna had discovered that Sally is on sick leave from the restaurant in Mayfair, so she went for a root around in her room. There's a lot more to tell you about Sally."

Horace didn't get the opportunity to say anything else because they heard someone coming in through the back door. Hercules leapt up and charged through into the annexe like something demented. They heard excited whining, followed by laughter and two voices.

Gina entered the kitchen, followed by Sally with Hercules nuzzling himself as close as he could get. Both women stopped in their tracks when they saw the trio staring open-mouthed.

Marjorie recovered first. "Good morning. It's good to have you back, Sally. Thank you for letting her in," she said to Gina.

Neither woman spoke, but their faces reddened like naughty schoolchildren.

"Tea?" suggested Horace. "I was just going to tell Marjorie about your relationship, but perhaps it would be better coming from you."

"Now I am intrigued," said Marjorie. "Please join us."

The two women sat down, thanking Horace, who had brought a fresh pot of tea over. Hercules didn't leave Sally's side, and it was she who spoke first.

"How much do you know?"

"I know quite a bit," said Horace, "but Marjorie and Fred are in the dark."

"We've had a very late night, so if you could try to be as clear as possible," said Marjorie, "I'd be most grateful."

Gina found her voice. "Sally's my daughter." She held the younger woman's hand protectively.

"I see," said Marjorie, recovering from the shock announcement. "Have you been playing some kind of trick on me?"

"No, Marjorie. I would never do anything like that," said Gina.

"She didn't know until yesterday," said Sally. "I told her while you were at the market, before… well, you know."

"Is that why you went to the police station, to cover up for your mother?" Frederick asked.

Sally nodded. "We were going to explain everything today, but after I found out about Marcus Singleton's death…" Marjorie noticed the change in tone when she mentioned the late man's name, "… I wasn't sure what had happened. Gina… Mum told me last night she had nothing to do with it."

"Please go back to the beginning because you're losing me already," said Marjorie, pouring herself another cup of tea.

"Right," said Sally. "The thing is, I've always known I was adopted. My adoptive parents were honest with me as soon as they thought I could understand. To be frank, I didn't care. They were… still are… great parents, but when

I came out of college and started working, I began digging around, looking for my birth parents.

"It's taken a few years and a DNA test to get to this point. The only thing is, I wasn't sure how they would respond. I did my research on Mum first because there was no father's name on the birth certificate. After more research, I tried to find out who my birth father was, but didn't get very far until I got here."

"And so, you took sick leave from your day job to meet your mother," Horace said.

Sally's chin dropped. "They don't know, do they? I could lose my job."

"I don't think so. It was Edna who found out, and she was quite discreet."

Doubt crossed Sally's face.

"My cousin can be circumspect when she wants to be. She won't have given you away," said Marjorie.

"How did she find out?" Sally asked.

"You're not the only detective around here," said Horace, winking.

"I take it your birth father was Marcus Singleton?" Marjorie said, looking at Gina.

"When did you find out?"

"Just this minute. I had one of those lightbulb moments. Gina… your reaction to meeting him the other day and Sally thinking you were responsible for killing him.

If you had, you wouldn't have let Sally take the blame. There are still some gaps you need to fill in, though. I don't want to pry, but as the man's dead, we need to know everything."

Frederick rubbed his bald head. "What about the police? Do they still think you did it?"

"They might. They're confused about who prepared his lunch yesterday."

"I'm not surprised," said Horace, with a twinkle in his eye. "Marjorie told them it was her, and then you, Sally, probably told them it was you."

It was Gina's turn to appear surprised, eyes widening. "Well, I'm going to tell them today that it was me."

"Poor Corbin Crow," said Marjorie, stifling a giggle.

"That's the detective inspector," Sally explained to her newfound mother before carrying on with her story. "When my mother found out she was pregnant, Marcus wouldn't do the honourable thing and marry her, so circumstances forced her into one of them birthing homes to give me away."

Marjorie felt a surge of compassion for her dear housekeeper. "That must have been very hard."

Gina's eyes filled with tears. "I was sixteen. He was twenty-one, and I was besotted. My parents knew nothing about the relationship or they would have forbidden it.

They wouldn't have been able to live with the shame of an unmarried mother for a daughter.

"Marcus had persuaded me to give myself up to him. He told me he loved me. When I discovered I was pregnant, I thought he'd do right by me, but he told me in no uncertain terms he wasn't interested. He threatened to tell my parents I'd been sleeping with other boys at school.

"Anyway, I called my aunt, who lived in Lincoln. She knew of a place called The Quarry, a maternity home where lots of single mothers gave birth before putting their babies up for adoption. I desperately wanted to keep her, but my aunt said she'd have a better life if I let her go.

"Bob has always known about this, even though we've not been able to have children of our own, and he's never thrown it in my face. As soon as Sally told me yesterday, I went home and told him."

"How did he react?" asked Frederick.

"He's philosophical, is my Bob. He took it all in his stride and said as long as I was happy, he would love to meet her. When she called late last night, I collected her from the station and she stayed the night."

"What does Bob know about Marcus Singleton?" Marjorie asked.

Gina's head dropped. "Nothing. I never told him the name of the man who caused me such pain. In fact, I never wanted to mention his name at all, and then he showed up the other day, calling himself Marcus."

"Yes, we have unearthed the fact his name is Mark, but for simplicity's sake and so you don't have to think of him as you knew him, we'll stick with Marcus," said Marjorie.

"Did he recognise you the other day?" Horace asked.

"Yes. At first, I thought not, but when he came to the kitchen later, he told me not to say a word or he'd ruin my reputation, such as it was. That's how he put it. I had no intention of raking up the past, and I told him so."

"Horrible man," said Marjorie.

"I saw the two of them arguing and heard what he said," Sally added. "That's when I realised he was my birth father, and as he'd rejected my mother without shame and was threatening her, I knew he wouldn't welcome a daughter."

"Which explains why you let Hercules terrorise him," said Marjorie, grinning.

"I was pretending to get something from a cupboard when he stormed past. He was ranting away, paying me no attention. When Hercules trapped him, I hid in the alcove, enjoying watching him cower."

"As I suspected. You realise, though, that the police will uncover all this information when they do their background checks, and will suspect one of you murdered him? Both of you had not only the opportunity, but also the motive to commit murder."

Gina's face was solemn. "I didn't hate him. That's what I tried to explain before he started threatening me. He meant nothing to me and I've been very happy with Bob. Of course, I didn't know then that Sally was my daughter or I might have felt differently."

"It's funny, Sally. When I first met you, I knew there was something familiar. You have your mother's kind and mischievous eyes," said Marjorie.

Both women smiled. "I'm sorry for coming here under false pretences, but I wanted to know whether my mother would want to know me."

Judging by the look of pride on Gina's face, Marjorie had the answer to that question.

"The guests will be getting up shortly. Do you think you could manage breakfast?"

"Definitely," said Sally. "I intend to fulfil my duties."

"You do that and, in the meantime, the rest of us ought to retreat to my sitting room to confer on how we're going to find the real killer before the police arrest half my household."

Horace guffawed. "Including you, Marjorie," he said.

Chapter 22

"Well, well, well," said Frederick. "I wouldn't have guessed any of that, but I knew a cook wouldn't be short of work at this time of year."

"She's actually a chef," said Horace, "who works at a posh restaurant in Mayfair called Prince's. The chance to meet her birth mother was obviously too much of an opportunity to miss, so knowing she wouldn't get the time off, she called in sick."

"Let's hope they don't find out," said Marjorie.

"Surely they would understand?" said Frederick.

"I doubt it. They will have been clamouring around to find a decent chef at short notice at their busiest time of year. You know as well as I do, Fred, business is business." Horace paced the floor, staring out of the window. "I wonder if I should take Edna some tea."

"That's a splendid idea," said Marjorie. "Why don't you check whether she's awake and we'll give her an update?"

"If I didn't know you better, I'd say Edna's growing on you," said Horace.

"I don't know what you mean," said Marjorie, stubbornly. "She's a guest in my house and I treat everyone the same."

Horace tapped his nose. "Don't worry, I won't tell her."

"Perhaps we should all go now before the others come down. In the light of what we've just discovered, we may need to open that briefcase."

Frederick paled. "I'm not sure we should do that."

"Where's your sense of adventure, Fred?" said Horace, slapping him on the back.

"I'd prefer not to spend Christmas in a prison cell, if that's okay with you," Frederick countered. Nevertheless, he accompanied them upstairs and Marjorie knocked on Edna's door.

"Come in," was shouted from inside. Marjorie opened the door and poked her head around it to check Edna was fit to be seen. "Could you give me a hand with this? It's lopsided." Edna was sitting up in bed with a short permed black wig flying at half-mast.

"Wait there a moment, gents," Marjorie said, scurrying across the room to the rescue.

Once the hair predicament had been attended to, Edna grinned. "I bet you didn't expect to see me here, did you?"

Marjorie didn't like to point out that she wouldn't have been knocking on Edna's door if she didn't know she was back. Instead, she said, "Horace and Frederick are waiting outside. Is it all right to call them in?"

"Feel free. Horace saw me at my worst last night. I bet you all had a good laugh about me wig being on the floor."

"Edna Parkinton! I would never do such a thing. We're your friends and you've given us quite a fright. The last thing on any of our minds was your hair issues, and Horace replaced it before anyone else saw anything." Marjorie opened the door. "Come on in," she said to the men. "She's quite decent. And back to her normal self."

"Hello, Edna. How are you feeling this morning?" Horace moved over to her, kissing her on the right cheek before sitting on the edge of the bed. Frederick pulled two chairs closer to the bed, and he and Marjorie sat down.

"I slept for a couple of hours. Them painkillers were like knockout drops, but I kept dreaming I was in pain before realising I was. This bloomin' arm's agony. I'd like to go back to that hospital and give that consultant a piece of my mind."

Horace snorted. "Trust me, Edna, you already did. Why do you think he let you come home rather than keeping you in?"

Edna joined in with his laughter. Watching the two of them with their heads thrown back, snorting with amusement, Marjorie felt an unexpected sense of joy.

"Ow! Stop now, it's making me shoulder hurt," said Edna.

"I'll get some tea while you fill her in on the latest," said Horace.

"Did he tell you what I found out?" Edna was preening.

"You did well, Edna. Sally's home now and she and Gina have just been telling us about their relationship."

Edna appeared slightly disappointed. "But I found out first."

"You certainly did. Horace told us how you found out Sally had called in sick. We didn't get to hear the rest because Sally and Gina came in, but I expect you discovered they were mother and daughter?"

"There was a photo of a young Gina and a bloke I recognised, along with a birth certificate and adoption records inside some sort of genealogy book. I put all the pieces together and worked out the bloke was Marcus and must have been the old flame, which would explain why Gina reacted to him when they met. Why are they downstairs? Surely it was one of them that killed Marcus Singleton?"

Horace arrived back with tea and poured Edna a mug while Marjorie told her everything Gina and Sally had told them downstairs.

"Who would have thought your starchy housekeeper had such skeletons in her cupboard, Marge?"

"We all have secrets, Edna. And my housekeeper is not starchy; she's efficient and good at her job, that's what she is."

"Okay, keep yer 'air on, Marge."

Marjorie opened her mouth to say something she might regret on the subject of hair, but Horace, thankfully, intervened.

"I found something else, Edna." He walked back to the end of the bed where he'd put the briefcase. "This was on the ground outside the study window. It must be what the person who knocked you over was trying to take."

Edna flinched at the recollection. "So, what's inside?"

Horace sat on the edge of the bed again, placing the briefcase on his knee. "We don't know. It's locked. I suspect the key was on Marcus's person when he died."

"Can't we force it?" Edna asked.

"That's what I was suggesting," said Marjorie.

"But if we do that, we'll be in trouble with the plods," said Horace.

Edna folded her arms, but yelped when she realised her left shoulder wasn't mended. Marjorie winced for her.

"I suggest you put that sling on. If only to serve as a reminder that you need to exercise more caution."

Blowing out her cheeks, Edna conceded. "I suppose you're right. If we're not going to open the briefcase, can I have breakfast in bed? I'm starving."

"Elsa should be in by now. I'll ask her to bring you something. It's good to have you back, Edna," said Marjorie.

"I didn't know you cared until I saw you crying last night," Edna replied.

Marjorie was walking towards the door, but turned her head. "I don't know what you mean. The cold brought tears to my eyes, that's all."

Edna and Horace cackled.

"Are you coming downstairs?" Marjorie said to the men. "We've got an outing to prepare for, remember, and we still have at least one crime to solve. We need to find out who locked Edna in my study and if they are one and the same person as the murderer."

"Marjorie's right," said Frederick, jumping up from the chair.

"What am I going to do?" Edna moaned.

"You're going to rest up. Sorry, old girl, but it looks like you'll be home alone today." Horace patted Edna on her good arm. Edna looked glum.

"I'll ask Elsa to pop in regularly," said Marjorie. "Actually, you could do something for us. If Horace leaves the briefcase here, you can call your new best friend, Inspector Crow, and tell him about it. After all, it might contain evidence pointing out who the actual killer is."

"Great idea, Marge. I'll also see if I can get him to tell me what's inside. We might have the case solved by the time you get back."

"Won't leaving the briefcase here put Edna in danger?" Horace sounded reluctant.

"Not if we make sure all the guests are with us," said Marjorie. "We can assume none of the staff is responsible."

"I've got an idea," said Frederick.

"Heavens above," said Edna. "I can't wait to hear this."

"Don't be sarcastic," said Horace. "What is it, Fred?"

"We can ask Sally if Hercules can stay with Edna as a sort of bodyguard."

"Or even a guard dog." Edna could drip sarcasm when she had a mind to. "But I suppose the beast will make me feel safe if you think it's necessary, as long as he keeps his smelly breath to himself."

"He was quite taken with you last night. You may not remember, but he kept you warm while we waited for the ambulance to arrive," Marjorie added.

"Why do you think I mentioned the stinky breath?"

"I'll feel better about going out if I know you're protected," said Horace. "We don't want anyone slipping back and having another go at getting that briefcase, do we? While I think of it, I'll push it under the bed so it's out of sight." Horace removed the briefcase from the bed and made sure the eiderdown was covering the space underneath it. Satisfied the briefcase was out of sight, he kissed Edna on the cheek and followed Frederick and Marjorie out of the room.

"I think you're all overreacting. I doubt anyone knows I have the case," called Edna.

Apart from the person who shoved you over, thought Marjorie, but kept it to herself.

Once they left Edna, she said, "That was a good idea, Frederick. I'd say she looked almost relieved."

"And putting the briefcase out of reach will stop her trying to do anything silly like having a go at opening it," said Horace. "Now, gang, it's time to catch a killer."

Chapter 23

Marjorie's mind was elsewhere over breakfast. Despite ruling out Gina and Sally, she still had too many suspects to narrow it down to one person, and it didn't help that Marcus Singleton had been so unpopular. If she were that way inclined, she might have wanted to kill him herself.

It was all about finding out who had a motive strong enough for them to want or need him out of the way. Which one of the people in this room would benefit the most from his demise, and was it business or personal? So many questions whizzed around her foggy head, but not enough answers.

Christina was, not surprisingly, quiet and she hardly ate a thing.

"Methinks someone has a hangover," Horace whispered in Marjorie's ear.

"Serves her right. I expect she's also embarrassed about making an exhibition of herself." Marjorie had been weighing up all that Christina had told her and Elsa the previous evening. Of all the guests, she was the only one who had a powerful motive that they knew of for killing Marcus, but then she herself had most likely been attacked.

"I've just had a thought," Marjorie said to Horace.

"What?"

Marjorie checked no-one was listening in on their conversation, but Colm was preoccupying them. He'd become their self-appointed travel guide and was making a list of what each of them wanted to do with their time in central London.

"We must make the most of it while we're here. After today, it's all business," he said.

Horace nudged Marjorie to bring her attention back to what she had been going to say.

"I wonder if the person who locked Edna in my study was the same one Christina heard when she went outside. Do you remember her saying she felt a pressure on her neck before she passed out? Perhaps that person had gone around the back of the house to retrieve the briefcase when she disturbed them."

Horace rubbed his forehead, whispering, "It explains why they left it. I expect they panicked once they caused her to pass out and carried her out of sight. That would also explain how she was found at the far end of your garden, away from the study window and the briefcase."

"Which rules Mary Anne out, because whoever moved Christina had to be strong enough to do so." Marjorie looked again at the rotund Christina Makepeace. "Frederick and Elsa struggled to get her up the stairs even when she was conscious."

"I know what you mean," said Horace. "Fred was whacked out after we brought her in last night. She's no lightweight. Although I like a woman with a bit of meat on her myself."

"Keep to the point, Horace," said Marjorie.

"I'd say it also rules Elmur out. He's no doubt strong, but he doesn't look fit enough to move much weight," said Horace. "Every time I see him, he's out of puff."

Marjorie switched her focus to Bruce and Colm. "Colm doesn't seem to have any reason to dislike Marcus, and if he had anything to do with it, Melissa would need to have been in on it, as they seem to be joined at the hip."

"Bruce told me he spends a lot of time at the gym when he's not doing business or playing sport." Horace sounded excited. "Plus, he's built like an all-in wrestler. He could be our man. The only thing is he doesn't have a motive."

"Not one we've discovered. He seems to get on well with Frederick. I suggest you and he make Bruce your target for today. I'll see what I can find out about Colm and Melissa, although I don't see either of them being responsible. Tell me… would someone who can make a person pass out by applying pressure to the neck need to be trained in the martial arts?"

Horace thought for a moment before replying, "Or the military, and they'd have to sneak up on someone without being heard in order to do so. It's looking more and more like we have our man with Bruce. Let's see what Fred and I can dig up."

Something was bothering Marjorie, but she couldn't quite put her finger on what it was. "If only we knew what was in that blessed briefcase."

"Of course, Marcus's death and the shove in the study could be unconnected," said Horace. "The person after the briefcase might have been taking advantage of his death rather than the one who caused it."

"I had thought of that too, but for now let's assume they are connected or my head will explode," said Marjorie. "And of course, the other big question is which one of these people would have access to potassium cyanide, because they didn't find it under the Christmas tree. Not that we have one yet."

Horace chuckled. "Nice one, Marjorie. I suppose anyone determined to get their hands on it could do so quite easily."

"How?"

"A weaker version of the stuff is in photo developing fluids, but it only needs to be mixed with a bit of acid to make it lethal. It's still used in industrial pest control, or the killer might have access to it from a laboratory. What is it these people are hoping to supply to Jeremy?"

"Some sort of metal components for manufacturing. I don't know the details."

"In which case, any of them could have access to cyanide salts if they use electroplating."

"Which is?"

"It's complicated, but basically, it's when a metal is coated using electrodes. In our firm, we had cyanide under lock and key, but these people are CEOs, so if they use electroplating themselves, or their companies do, they'll have access to cyanide."

"Which gives them means and, most likely, the opportunity. It wouldn't have been difficult to add a lethal dose to Marcus's flask before leaving yesterday morning. But what we need now is motive."

They didn't have time to discuss the matter any further as Faith arrived. Nobody had asked about Edna, but then again, she sometimes grated on people so they might have been pleased she wasn't there, or assumed she was having breakfast in bed.

One of them, however, had every reason to be wondering whether Edna had found the briefcase and what had happened to it. Of course, Marjorie and her friends were all assuming there was something incriminating in Marcus's briefcase, but it might turn out to be of little or no use. Unless Marcus had told whoever his killer was that he had something he could use against them.

Did each of her guests have something to hide? Marjorie was back to her original question: which one had a secret so big they would kill to keep it hidden?

Chapter 24

While the guests readied themselves for the day out, Marjorie debated with herself whether she should sit this one out and stay home to look after Edna. It would also give her the opportunity to see what the DI had to say about the briefcase. In the back of her mind, she worried he'd bulldoze his way into arresting her housekeeper once he discovered it was she who had prepared Marcus's lunch and she had a damning motive for killing the man who had caused her so much pain. Poor Gina. What a burden she had borne all these years. It would be awful to have her newfound joy taken away by an overzealous policeman.

"I heard what happened to Edna. How is she?" Faith interrupted Marjorie's musings.

"You know Edna. She's as strong as a horse. I'm sorry to have dragged you away from your mother again when so much is going on here."

Faith smirked. "It's a welcome diversion, believe me. If we are together for too long, we get on each other's nerves. I'm not allowed out of her sight when I'm staying with her, but the neighbours assure me she's fine when I'm not there."

"Nobody's above a bit of emotional blackmail, although I really appreciate you giving up your time to help, even if it is welcome. I hope Colm hasn't upset your plans for the day with his extra demands."

"Not at all. I've called in a favour from an old friend, so we have the use of a minibus for the day. Nick knows all the hidden parking spots in and around London, so we'll be fine."

"You are a wonder. I was debating whether I should stay here and keep an eye on Edna." Marjorie didn't mention her other concerns.

"I can understand that, but there's no need. Horace has just told me he's going to stay behind."

Drat, thought Marjorie, but said, "In that case, where are we heading?"

"We'll start with Madame Tussauds, because I've managed to get us tickets, then we're going to the London Eye. Bruce and a few of the others are going to take a speedboat trip while the rest of us go on the Eye, and then we'll have lunch at The Hard Rock Café in Marble Arch before finishing the day at Harrods for a bit of shopping."

Marjorie was pleased to hear about the lunch arrangements. In view of the poisoning, she hadn't asked Sally to provide luncheon.

"My goodness. It sounds as though we are in for a busy day. My head's spinning at the thought." Marjorie already felt exhausted from the previous day's events, but it seemed her guests' holiday mood was only just beginning. "Has anyone tried to bow out?"

"Other than Horace, no. Although Christina looks peaky and says she might not last the duration. I heard all about her antics last night. Apparently she's got a slight ankle sprain."

"Oh, I forgot to ask her about that. She had a fall in the garden."

"Yes, she told me, and Mary Anne told me the rest." Faith winked. "But don't worry, she seems as keen as anyone to tour London. I get the feeling none of them want to miss out, but I don't know whether that's to avoid backhand deals being brokered while they're not looking or because they're keen to see London at Christmastime. I can't promise we won't get stuck in traffic jams, but we're in safe hands with Nick."

Marjorie noticed a sparkle in Faith's eye and a slight blushing underneath the makeup when she mentioned his name, making her wonder whether Nick was an old – or new – flame.

"I'm looking forward to it already, but I think I'll give the speedboat a miss."

Faith laughed. "You're not the only one."

Noticing most of the guests were putting coats on, Marjorie said, "If you'll excuse me for a moment, I'd better have a quick word with Edna before I leave."

Horace was already in Edna's room when Marjorie arrived. He was reading a copy of the *Financial Times* while Edna was doing something on her tablet. Hercules gave a little tail wag and a snort.

"That dog is made for you two," said Marjorie.

"What do you mean?" Edna looked up from whatever it was she was doing.

"Never mind."

"Am I in trouble?" Horace asked. "I'm sorry, Marjorie. It didn't feel right leaving her here on her own. Elsa and the temps are going to be busy cleaning and tidying and helping Sally."

"You're not in any bother with me. I was going to do the same until Faith told me you were staying behind."

"I'm touched," said Edna, grinning.

"Don't read too much into it," said Marjorie before turning to Horace. "Did you ask Frederick to focus on Bruce?"

"Yes, I did. They get on well. He'll be better at it than me. I can't take to the fellow; all he talks about is having a good time, going to the gym and women."

Marjorie felt the last point would be right up Horace's street, but didn't say so. "I suspect he's more ambitious than he lets on. I don't like his eyes," she said.

"I know what you mean," agreed Horace, "dark and unflinching."

"Quite," said Marjorie.

"I hear you've got quite a marathon ahead of you, Marge. Are you sure you're up to it?" Edna clearly couldn't resist a poke.

"I'll let you know when I get back. Bruce has arranged for a few of the guests to go out on a Thames speedboat ride."

"Heavens," said Horace.

"Blimey, Marge. You won't be trying that, will you?"

"You'll have to wait and see, won't you?"

"She's joking, Edna," said Horace, noticing Edna's goldfish impression.

"Oh, right. Well, you remember to take your stick, Marge."

"I'm quite capable of walking without it," said Marjorie.

"Yeah, right," said Edna, adding, "Please be careful. One of them's a killer."

"I will. I hope you get on okay with Inspector Crow. With any luck, he'll have the affable sergeant with him. I'll see you later." Hercules let out a snorty sigh. "And you, Hercules. Look after them both."

"See you later, Marge. I'll give Corbin Crow a ring as soon as you've gone," said Edna.

Marjorie was still grinning when she put on her hat and coat before leaving the house. Her grin widened as she took a sturdy walking stick from the holder and descended the steps to the minibus. Edna would never know.

Chapter 25

Bruce had paired up with Elmur, sitting just in front of Marjorie and Frederick in the minibus. Christina, wearing a headscarf and dark glasses, was sitting at the front on her own, with Colm and Melissa behind her. Mary Anne occupied another front seat and Faith sat next to her.

Marjorie tried to listen in on Bruce and Elmur's conversation, but they were talking about business strategy. After eavesdropping for a while, she realised Bruce was doing more fishing and less talking than Elmur.

"He's trying to keep Elmur's mind off the money markets," Frederick whispered.

"And succeeding," said Marjorie, who wasn't convinced Bruce's intentions were as benevolent as Frederick thought, but she couldn't be sure whether her suspicions were because she now considered him a murder suspect. Bruce certainly had the physique of a person who could have moved Christina with ease. He had leapt to the top of her list.

"Who's your key contact for European business?" Marjorie heard Bruce ask. Elmur freely delivered the names of several contacts and Marjorie couldn't help thinking Bruce was making a mental note of them, suspecting he was ruthless enough to steal work from Elmur. The latter was vulnerable to losing his business if his gambling was as serious a problem as it appeared to be. She had a sudden desire to warn Elmur that his newfound friend might not be all he seemed. She toyed with the idea of asking Jeremy to offer the Welshman the contract, but that was her heart speaking, not her head. Unless Elmur acknowledged he had a problem and sought help for it, his business and most likely his marriage were doomed.

Marjorie had witnessed over the years how businesses that showed promise at the beginning could fail or succeed on the whims, weaknesses or strengths of their founders. It was a depressing thought, but like any addiction, gambling was destructive and unscrupulous people could easily manipulate an addict. Bruce was easy going on the surface, but something about him sent warning bells ringing through Marjorie's head. Horace had compounded her suspicion: it was in the eyes.

Her musings returned to Marcus's death, and she wondered whether Elmur could have been desperate enough to kill him. Elsa had told Edna how he had been summoned to see Marcus, and Marjorie had no doubt Marcus's intention would have been to exploit the man's weakness. From the little she knew and had seen of Marcus, he would have had no qualms about resorting to blackmail. Gambling aside, Elmur was an affable man, apart from showing his impatience with Jeremy the night before. He appeared to have an innocence, or what Ralph would have called a decent streak. Was he capable of killing a man to protect his marriage and his business? He had boasted about his children's achievements and most likely wouldn't want their chances in life damaged by his loss of status.

Perhaps she was being too hasty in suspecting Bruce based on physical fitness alone. After all, he was one of the few who didn't appear to have any motive. Or did he? Something he'd said was in the back of her mind, niggling to get out, but she couldn't recall what it was.

"You're very quiet," Frederick interrupted her thoughts.

"I was cogitating. It's a habit of old age."

"You don't have to tell me. I'm the world's worst when it comes to that habit. The problem is, it can lead you down all sorts of mazes, don't you find?"

"Yes, you're right," she agreed.

The minibus pulled up in front of the famous Madame Tussauds, and they all stepped onto the pavement and huddled around in a group. A huge queue she couldn't see the end of made Marjorie's heart sink.

"Don't tell me we've got to join that," said Mary Anne with a look of despair on her face.

"Follow me," called Faith, leading them to another much smaller queue for those who already had tickets.

"Where did you find that woman? She's an absolute genius," said Colm, sidling up behind Marjorie and Frederick. Marjorie felt a sense of pride at knowing Faith Weathers. She was a wonder, a born leader, excellent at her job with a natural affinity for people. Faith was perfect for what she did.

"We met on a river cruise from Amsterdam. If you ever want to take your family on holiday, find out which tours Faith is leading and you won't be disappointed," Marjorie said, unable to resist mentioning his absent family. Colm didn't even blush. Instead, he grinned.

"I might just do that."

There was a devious man who openly paraded his infidelity for all to see, but did his wife know about the affair? And if not, could that be something Marcus might have used to wield power over the ice-cool Colm McCleary? Marjorie's head ached from all the possibilities

238

and suspects. She was no closer to the truth than she had been before settling on Bruce as the perpetrator.

Once inside the waxworks, Faith led the sightseers through to see various exhibits, including models of the royal family and characters from the Star Wars franchise. Frederick reluctantly joined Bruce and Elmur for the House of Horrors whilst Marjorie tried to inspire her inner detective by participating in an interactive Sherlock Holmes experience. So focused on following the clues was she, she didn't realise Christina and Mary Anne were tagging along a few feet behind until she was about halfway through. Rather than participating, though, they were having a hushed conversation between themselves. Marjorie assumed they were plotting a business proposal to put to Jeremy this evening, although they could be talking about Christina's revelations from the night before. Perhaps she was asking just how much she had stepped out of line.

Marjorie smiled, recalling how embarrassed Frederick had been by the uninhibited woman's innuendo and how quickly he had retreated. Christina was walking without a limp this morning; her ankle couldn't be troubling her anymore, so no real harm had come from her experience in the garden. Marjorie wondered again at who could have caused her to faint, and then carried or dragged her away. What would they have done if Hercules hadn't interrupted? She assumed nothing more. The intruder hadn't attacked Edna, other than to push her out of the way so they could lock her in Marjorie's study. They were unlikely to kill again, unless... Marjorie paused for a moment, looking at a clue in the Sherlock experience, but not studying it closely... unless the person was in danger of being exposed.

What was surprising was the fact they had made no further attempt to retrieve the briefcase. If whoever locked Edna in Marjorie's study and then attacked Christina was concerned there might be evidence inside, it made no sense to leave it outside.

Marjorie shook her head, annoyed that this complex case wasn't offering any real clues for her to follow. She pretended to be enthralled by the Holmes clue while the two women passed her, listening in to what they were saying.

"I'd love to know who bumped the man off. I'd buy them a drink," said Christina, whose hangover didn't seem to trouble her any longer. She had removed the dark glasses.

"Me too," said Mary Anne.

"Oh really? I wondered whether you two had history when you weren't on the original list. You should have seen Marcus's face when he set eyes on you. Are you going to tell me what that was all about?" Christina shuffled

Mary Anne to one side. Marjorie hung back, trying to hear above the chatter of a group of tourists and the exhibition actors directing them on to their next clue. She craned her neck, thankful for being small, which gave her the opportunity to hide behind a tall and burly woman.

"It's no big secret. Marcus – which, as you know, wasn't his real name – didn't want me involved because I know him of old."

"How?"

"I hate to admit it, but we were married once."

The silence that followed indicated Christina Makepeace was as shocked as Marjorie on hearing this news. Marjorie couldn't quite see them, so she shuffled behind a wax image of a policeman when the tall woman moved on. She wondered if they had gone on themselves, but then heard Christina speak again.

"You kept that one close to your chest. I wouldn't have guessed if you'd given me weeks to work it out."

"I was young and foolish and fell for his charm. He was always a good looker, but there was nothing else good about him. He's had two wives since me and was alone again, from what I heard."

"Who divorced who?" Christina asked.

"I divorced him. It would never have lasted, but it hurt his ego. I don't know how he found out my second marriage name was Beider, but once he did, he rescinded my invite and told me I wasn't welcome. Once upon a time, I would have accepted it and been afraid to challenge him, but those days are long gone, so I called Jeremy. He and I have met in the past and I know our company is exactly what he needs."

"What did you say?"

"I told him straight that Marcus and I had a history which he couldn't let go of and assured him there was no bitterness on my part, and I was more than willing to strike a working relationship with the man if that's what it took to get the contract."

"You think the contract's yours, do you? We'll have to see about that." Christina had clearly realised the implications of what Mary Anne had shared from the business angle, which she had missed when focusing on the gossip.

Mary Anne laughed. "There's room for more than one company. Perhaps we should strike a deal and put the proposal to Jeremy. We can work together to oust the fellas."

Christina cackled, which rang out in the cavelike area they stood in. Marjorie decided it was time to leave them to their scheming and hid herself amongst a large group making its way through the exhibits.

Once she had finished the tour, she found Frederick waiting for her. He was breathless with excitement.

"You're going to want to hear what I've found out," he gasped.

"I have news too. Shall we sneak away for a coffee while the others finish their walkthrough?"

Chapter 26

There wasn't a café as such in Madame Tussauds, but Marjorie and Frederick found a fondue station serving ice cream and treats. Frederick was hopping up and down, barely able to contain himself by the time they had reached the front of the queue to get their drinks and chocolate fondues. The area wasn't too busy, as most people seemed to grab drinks on the go from stations strategically placed throughout the building.

Frederick checked his watch. "We have to meet Faith outside in twenty minutes."

"How was the House of Horrors?" Marjorie asked.

"Not as horrible as I had imagined, but bad enough."

"What is it you found out from Bruce and Elmur?"

"Nothing." Frederick seemed to have lost his sense of purpose and was tucking into the fondue. Marjorie waited patiently for him to finish a mouthful.

"But you found out something, presumably from someone else?"

"Horace phoned me. They've been trying to call you, but—"

"I don't carry a phone around with me when I'm in London." *Or anywhere else, for that matter*, remained unsaid.

"Precisely," said Frederick. He lowered his voice. "Elmur's going to steal one of your paintings."

Marjorie did a double take, shocked to the core. "I don't believe it," she said once she recovered. "You must be confused. Christina told me last night it was Marcus Singleton who was the art thief."

"I realise the idea is appalling, Marjorie, but they've got evidence."

"The police have opened the briefcase, then?" Marjorie's head was still reeling at the thought that someone she was hosting in her own home would consider stealing from her. And she was deeply disappointed in Elmur, whom she had taken a liking to despite his inclination for gambling.

"No, they don't know what's in the briefcase yet. As far as I'm aware, the DI is dragging his heels and hasn't even been back to the house yet. He told Horace he has too much serious crime to contend with to jump to attention at the whim of people playing amateur detectives."

"I can imagine Corbin Crow saying that. If we don't sort this out soon, he'll arrest Gina when he finds out who really prepared the man's lunch. You haven't said how Horace – and, I assume, Edna – discovered this evidence."

Frederick's face went scarlet as he finished his fondue. "When we were on the minibus, I texted Horace and suggested it might be an excellent opportunity for him to look inside the guests' rooms once the agency staff finished cleaning them."

Marjorie's jaw dropped. "Normally I would ask why I didn't think of that, but these are people staying under my roof. It doesn't sit well with me."

"Are you angry with me?"

"Just tell me what you know."

"Only what I told you. I couldn't stay on the phone with Horace because I was with Elmur and Bruce. I told them I needed the loo, and that's when I bumped into you."

"Let's call him now, then," said Marjorie. "I would like to know what they have discovered."

"We haven't got time," said Frederick. "We'll have to wait until the next stop. I'm not going on the London Eye and I've no intention of getting on a speedboat, so we'll see if we can find the time to ring him then. I'll text him now to let him know."

Marjorie felt nothing but frustration and disappointment while Frederick tapped into his phone. It was bad enough having a murder to solve without finding out one of Jeremy's guests was planning to steal from her, and that Horace and most likely Edna were rooting through her visitors' rooms. It really was too much. She rubbed her temples, trying to relax.

"We certainly don't have time to ring Horace now. Here they come," said Frederick.

Marjorie turned to find Bruce and Elmur walking towards them.

"We wondered where you'd got to," Elmur's Welsh lilt would normally have sounded pleasant to her ear, but right now it was infuriating. Marjorie couldn't bring herself to look at him.

"I bumped into Marjorie, so we took a break," Frederick said, flushing again. He really wasn't very good at subterfuge, but hopefully the men would misinterpret his embarrassment as being for leaving them to have refreshments.

"It's time to go. We saw the others heading out to meet Faith and I think her guy can only make a brief stop to pick us up," Bruce said. "Are you all right, Marjorie? You seem tense."

"I'm fine, thank you. It must have been my Sherlock Holmes experience. It was quite realistic, you know." Marjorie finished her tea and allowed Frederick to pull her chair back. How she found the strength to get outside with her legs feeling like jelly, she didn't know, but she was determined not to allow this latest revelation to distract her from preventing her good friend and housekeeper from being accused of murder. Perhaps Elmur was the culprit after all.

Faith was waiting outside, and it seemed like just a few minutes later they were deposited near the London Eye. Neither Marjorie nor Frederick's plans went the way they had wanted them to, as Bruce cajoled Frederick and half-dragged him onto the waiting speedboat because they needed one more passenger. Sighing, Marjorie joined the others as they hurried to climb aboard one of the famous pods of the London Eye. The excitement was palpable as they made their way to the giant Ferris wheel, eager to get a bird's-eye view of the city. Marjorie was carried away in the moment, but couldn't help feeling nervous as she stepped inside the last pod, encouraged by Faith to join her. When the wheel turned and they rose higher and higher into the air, Marjorie's heart raced with anticipation.

"How's it going so far?" asked Faith.

Marjorie didn't know how much to say, but felt that this might be her only chance of privacy enough to call Horace.

She gazed out at the familiar skyline before looking at the sprawling metropolis below, taking in the vibrant energy of the place.

Refocusing on Faith, she said, "I assume you're referring to our little investigation. I've discovered some disturbing news. Would you mind terribly if I borrowed your phone to call Horace?"

Faith offered a supportive smile. "Have you found out who killed Marcus?"

"I don't think so," said Marjorie, "it's more of a personal matter."

"Of course, you can use my phone." Faith removed it from her handbag. "I'll even tap in the number for you. There you go, it's ringing."

Faith returned to the view while Marjorie waited for Horace to answer.

"Hello, Faith, how's the trip?"

"It's not Faith, it's Marjorie. I'm using her telephone because Bruce and Elmur have persuaded Frederick to board a speedboat. I do hope he'll be all right."

"Blimey! He's brave."

"That's not helping."

"He'll be fine, Marjorie. I suppose he told you what we found out, then?"

"A little, but I'm not sure how I feel about you and Edna rifling through the guest rooms. I hope you're putting things back as you find them."

"Sorry, Marjorie, but Fred's idea made sense. It's the perfect opportunity."

"I think you had better tell me what you've found," she said.

"So far, we've only gone through Bruce and Elmur's rooms. We found nothing in Bruce's. He appears to be everything he says he is: a fitness fanatic who runs a successful business. As far as we could see, there was nothing linking him to Marcus Singleton and no poison in the room." Horace guffawed.

"I see," said Marjorie, not quite so amused.

"There is one thing, though: his girlfriend owns an art gallery. There are photos of the two of them outside for a grand opening."

"That's what I've been trying to remember. He mentioned it last night, but I doubt it has any bearing on Marcus's death."

"Unless Bruce acted as a fence between Marcus and his girlfriend. We couldn't access his laptop, which could contain more secrets, but he obviously uses a more secure password than Elmur does."

Marjorie felt her breath catch. "Please don't tell me you've looked on Elmur's computer?"

"It wasn't difficult. The man doesn't even use a password and has an ancient laptop with no security. I guess he uses his phone for more important things."

"More important than stealing my paintings, you mean?"

Faith's head shot away from the view and her mouth opened.

"We found nothing about that on his computer either. He had photos of the Thomas Kinkade hanging in your sitting room hidden inside an envelope in his bedside table drawer."

"That doesn't prove he was going to steal it." Marjorie felt more hopeful.

"With it was a printout of a search for estimates if the piece were to go to private collectors not too concerned about dealing with stolen property, with notes by each one. And there was a photo of Bruce Melville and his girlfriend outside her art gallery. What if Elmur is stealing art and Bruce is acting as a fence?"

"All that tells us for now is that he has researched the painting's value and, at worst, he might consider taking it. It's a far cry from actually doing so. He's getting on well with Bruce, so the photo could be perfectly innocent. Besides, it would be too obvious for any of them to steal from me. The police would be on to them in no time."

"That's what Edna said," Horace admitted.

"For once, I agree with her. I'll bear this in mind, but I suspect Elmur Cartwright is prone to flights of fancy when he's lost too much on the currency markets or whatever it is he throws his money at. I don't think he's likely to carry out this act."

"There is something else," said Horace.

Marjorie's heart beat faster again. "Which is?"

"He has a book on poisons."

Marjorie almost dropped the phone. Faith helped her catch it, concern filling her compassionate eyes.

"Now that's different," Marjorie said once the telephone was securely within her grip. "Why didn't you say that in the first place?"

"How's he behaving today?"

Marjorie thought Elmur had seemed more at ease this morning than he had last night. It must have helped to know Marcus Singleton was out of the way and perhaps he'd moved into a winning streak for a change.

"Quite chipper, now I think of it."

"I think we have our man then, Marjorie. Art thief or not, he must be our killer. Everyone knows about his gambling troubles and how Marcus pulled him into a private meeting yesterday morning. Edna said he told Singleton he would not stand for it any longer and hours later, Singleton's dead."

"People can surprise and horrify you, can't they?" Marjorie said. "I felt sorry for him earlier. Why didn't you tell Frederick about the book?"

"We only found it after I phoned Fred. Edna found it hidden under Elmur's mattress."

The pod Marjorie and Faith were in had drawn to a halt.

"I have to go, Horace. Good luck telling Corbin Crow – if he ever turns up – about this fresh evidence and how you found it! In fact, don't mention it or he'll accuse you of planting it to protect Gina—"

The phone went dead as the signal was interrupted.

Chapter 27

Horace and Edna had been through all the rooms, but not found anything of any significance except implications that Elmur was planning to steal one of Marge's paintings and a poisons book.

"I've had enough of this," she said. "Let's get some lunch."

Thankfully, Horace didn't argue. After their finds in Elmur's room, they were both convinced he had poisoned Marcus Singleton, and Horace was still determined Elmur was planning to steal a painting too. A photo of Bruce Melville with his girlfriend at the opening of an art gallery suggested he might be working with Elmur, or vice versa.

The temporary staff were leaving when Edna and Horace arrived on the ground floor. A red-headed woman was writing a message on a notepad when she looked up and saw them.

"Oh, thank heavens. I'm running late to collect my daughter from my mother. Could you tell Mrs Makepeace I haven't managed to find her earring, but I'll have another look when I get back this evening?"

"Fine," said Edna, sniggering. "I guess she lost it last night, did she?"

"I think she must have. She was looking for it this morning after breakfast. I got the impression she thought one of us had stolen it. What good would one earring be to anybody?"

Edna checked the woman's name badge. "Don't you worry about her, Pippa. She can't go around blaming other people for her losing things when she's had too much to drink. You get off and collect your daughter."

"Thanks. It wouldn't be the first time we got the blame for items going missing, but they usually show up later, so we have the last laugh."

"She's right, you know," said Horace after Pippa had left. "I wouldn't do that job. It's the easiest thing in the world for people to blame temporary staff for things like that. If anything's gone missing, Christina only has herself to blame. I'll have a word with her when she gets back."

"Somehow, I can't imagine you in the uniform. Now, Mr Galahad, please find me some lunch."

Horace chortled. "Take my arm and I'll guide you to the kitchen. I'm sure Sally will rustle us up something."

Hercules was delighted to see Horace and Edna enter the kitchen, having been banished from Edna's bedroom when they went on their room search. He sneaked in from the annexe corridor and nuzzled against Edna's leg.

"Okay, Hercules. You're growing on me, but you still stink," she said, patting him on the head.

Sally grinned at them. "I was going to deliver you some lunch, but Elsa told me you were busy elsewhere."

Horace looked sheepish. It wouldn't take much for the watchful Elsa to work out what they were both up to, although they had tried hard to avoid her.

"Sorry," he said.

Twenty minutes later, Edna and Horace were devouring a wonderful winter vegetable soup with fresh stonebaked bread.

"This is marvellous," said Edna. "You must give me the recipe."

"Gladly," said Sally. "Did you find anything?"

"What do you mean?" Edna tried to play innocent.

"It's in mine and Gina – Mum's – interest to find this killer, you know."

Suddenly, Elsa and Gina appeared and joined them at the table. Horace guffawed.

"There's no hiding from these sleuths, Edna. We'll have to come clean."

"We think we know who killed Marcus," said Edna. "Did you notice anyone interfering with his flask after you filled it?" She aimed her question at Gina.

"What flask?" The housekeeper looked confused.

"The drinks flask you prepared for Marcus," said Horace.

"I didn't give him a flask," she said. "None of us did."

"She's telling the truth. He told me he had his own and that he only wanted lunch," said Elsa.

Realisation suddenly dawned on Sally, and then Gina. Mother and daughter hugged each other.

"So, the poison was in his flask? Thank God," said Gina. "I mean—"

"Don't worry," said Horace, "we know what you mean. All this time you had an alibi. Didn't the police ask you about the flask last night, Sally?"

"They did, but until this minute, I thought Mum had prepared it, so I told them I did his lunch and drink." Sally's eyes shone bright. "Now I have two witnesses to say I didn't do either, and Elsa can confirm that Mum didn't do the flask."

"I still don't understand why the police let you go," said Edna.

"It was after I told them anyone could have interfered with the drinks once they left the kitchen. Plus, I don't think the sergeant believed me, anyway. She said Lady Marjorie had told them she prepared lunch and wanted to know who we were all trying to protect."

At that moment, the doorbell rang. Gina went to answer it and returned a few minutes later with a gruff-looking DI Crow along with his DS. Hercules gave a low growl, stopping the inspector in his tracks.

"I suggest you approach calmly, Corbin," said Edna, laughing. "He doesn't like alpha males."

Maria Ouloupis's lips were upturned as she spoke. "We've been concluding our background checks and have discovered why you might wish to protect Mrs Ratton here, Sally."

"I was protecting her. But now I've found out it wasn't her who prepared Singleton's flask."

DI Crow didn't look happy with this revelation. "Says who?"

"Says I," said Gina.

"We've only just found out ourselves," said Edna. "Gina only prepared his sandwiches. He brought his own flask. I'm sure you can compare it to the ones the other guests took, which should clear the matter up."

"He could have asked her to fill it," said DI Crow, sulking.

"But he didn't," said Elsa. "I've just told them. I served him tea in Marjorie's study, and he told me he would need sandwiches for lunch. I asked if he wanted coffee or tea and he said he had his own flask of tonic water. He said it was for his gout."

"I've heard tonic water's good for gout," said Horace. "I have a friend who swears by it."

DI Crow let out a loud harrumph. "Perhaps we could ask you some further questions in private," he said to Elsa.

"No problem," she said. "I was going to have my lunch in the library, anyway. Would you like to join me?"

"This is hardly a social call," said the DI. "May I remind you all someone is dead? I've a good mind to charge you all with wasting police time."

Hercules gave a warning growl, and the DI retreated slowly.

"Would you mind?" Maria asked Elsa.

"Let's get on with it!" DI Crow yelled from a safe distance.

Once they had left, the four people remaining in the kitchen burst into fits of giggles. Then Horace tapped into his phone.

"I'd better text Fred and tell him the plods are here."

Chapter 28

During the drive to The Hard Rock Café, Marjorie could not speak to Frederick, who sat at the front of the bus holding a sick bag in front of him. Bruce and Elmur had tapped him on the back as they passed, with Bruce apologising. Although Marjorie sat beside Frederick while Christina, Mary Anne, Colm and Melissa moved further back, she couldn't speak without being overheard by the driver. Not that Frederick looked in a condition to have any sort of conversation.

Marjorie was feeling cross with Bruce Melville for forcing Frederick on his reckless trip along the Thames in the first place when a thought struck her. What if Bruce was indeed a fence, as Horace had suggested, and was going to act as one for Elmur? That would explain why the two men spent so much time together. Perhaps Marcus had been a third party, but got too greedy or wanted to keep her painting for himself.

What she couldn't understand was why Elmur would incriminate himself by keeping a book on poisons next to his bed. Surely he would expect the police to search the rooms for evidence. Or perhaps he was cleverer than he looked and had discovered Marcus and Gina's history and planned to frame her all along.

Marjorie's head was spinning by the time they were dropped off outside the restaurant. Once inside, it was made even worse. The venue was aptly named and she couldn't hear herself think. Frederick had disappeared inside the gents, looking extremely pale.

Faith appeared by her side. "Are you okay, Marjorie?"

Marjorie could barely hear her above the din, but managed a nod.

"We're over there." Faith pointed to tables in the far corner below an exhibition dedicated to John Lennon. "I'll try to get this over with as soon as possible, but the atmosphere's great in here." Faith was already swaying to the music and the rest of the party was seated and having fun. To be fair, rock music wasn't Marjorie's favourite at the best of times, and it wasn't the venue's fault that she had received alarming news and just wanted to put a killer where they belonged.

"Don't worry about me, I'll be fine," she tried to sound more reassuring than she felt. "I'll be along in a moment."

Not wanting to hover outside the gents' toilets, Marjorie waited near the entrance until she saw Frederick coming out again. His colour was better.

"Sorry about that," he said when he saw her. "I should have refused."

"They didn't give you much choice, from where I was standing. I think you were very brave to go at all."

Frederick's face brightened. "Do you really? If I was one of those alpha males Hercules doesn't take to, I'd say it was nothing, but to be honest, it was awful."

"How do you feel now?"

"Much better. I don't think Elmur liked the boat ride, but he pretended to."

Marjorie tensed at the mention of Elmur. "I spoke to Horace, but there's no point trying to shout above this noise. I'll fill you in as soon as I can."

"Righto," said Frederick. "Perhaps we'd better get over there. It looks like they're ready to order."

Marjorie saw Bruce and Mary Anne waving them over. "Whose choice was this place?"

"One guess," said Frederick, laughing.

"Bruce," she said.

Frederick smiled. "The others seem to like it, though. Look at them."

He was right. Mary Anne and Christina were swaying from side to side while Colm was entertaining them with his own rendition of whatever song was playing.

"Christina's hangover appears to be better," said Marjorie.

Lunch was tasty, and it didn't take Marjorie too long to adapt to hearing garbled conversations over the noise. She was pleased she didn't need hearing aids, despite Edna teasing her over the phone that her hearing might need testing. There was nothing wrong with it, but she had to admit that when it came to listening to Edna, she had a tendency to tune in and out, giving the impression of a problem. Although Edna rarely listened, so she was hardly one to talk.

"Thanks for bringing us here," said Mary Anne. "I love it."

"I think it's Bruce and Faith you have to thank," said Marjorie. She wondered where Nick went with the minibus while they were inside. Marble Arch was hardly a place blessed with parking – not cheap parking anyhow. She must ask Faith about paying him for his services when she found the time. The least she could do was cover a day's wages and the London congestion charge.

"I already have, but you've been a good sport taking us out these past two days. You must love Jeremy very much to do this for him the week before Christmas."

Marjorie was typical of the British aristocracy when it came to discussing feelings, especially with strangers, so she was grateful when Christina shouted something to interrupt the conversation. Besides, right now Marjorie felt like throttling her son, so what did that say about love? She chuckled to herself.

Just when Marjorie had got used to the loud music playing in the background, Faith called a halt to proceedings, advising the party that if they wanted to get to Harrods and back to Marjorie's before rush hour, it was time to leave.

Nick and his minibus were waiting for them when they arrived outside. Marjorie was pleased to witness an intimate meeting of eyes between him and Faith, confirming that he could well be a boyfriend, or soon to be so. Frederick sat beside Marjorie again, but this time, he was well enough to talk.

"I've just found a text from Horace, sent about an hour ago." He showed her his screen.

"Tell Marjorie the plods have arrived. They're talking to Elsa."

Marjorie's heart sank. "That silly man Corbin Crow is going to arrest Gina, isn't he?"

"Hang on, here's another one." Frederick read the text, and then showed Marjorie the screen again, asking, "What does this mean?"

Marjorie read the message. *"Crow is convinced the poison book is a plant. We need to talk to Marjorie."*

"This really is too much." She folded her arms across her chest. All she wanted to do was to get home and drum some sense into the stubborn DI.

"What does he mean?"

"I can't tell you now."

"What should I say?" Frederick asked.

"Ask him to delay the police and tell them we're on our way home."

Marjorie got up and walked to the front of the minibus, determined. Faith was still corralling the stragglers Colm, Melissa and Bruce in the vehicle's direction. Marjorie took Faith to one side and held a private conversation.

Once back on board, she rejoined Frederick, who raised both eyebrows. Then Faith did as Marjorie had asked and pretended to take a telephone call before calling for the group to settle down.

"I'm sorry, folks, there's been an accident blocking off the main roads to Harrods. I suggest we return to Marjorie's and try again another day if Jeremy can spare you."

There was surprisingly little reaction from the minibus passengers, who accepted the explanation with good grace.

"Nice one, Marjorie," Frederick said, winking.

Chapter 29

Gina Ratton opened the door before Marjorie could retrieve the key from her handbag. Marjorie grinned at the welcoming committee of Gina, Elsa and Edna.

"There are hot drinks, mulled wine and cakes in the reception room," Gina said once everyone was inside.

"Ooh, I could do with a coffee," said Mary Anne, removing her coat and handing it to Gina.

"Me too," said Christina. "Lunch was excellent, but we didn't have time for a hot drink afterwards."

As Gina took Christina's coat, Edna said, "I was asked to give you a message from Pippa, one of Marge's temps. She couldn't find your earring on the landing. It might be better to look in the garden tomorrow when it's light. I understand they found you in the grounds last night, so you must have lost it then." Edna had a steely gaze in her eye.

Christina frowned. "The earrings were a wedding gift from my mother. As well as being worth a lot of money, they are priceless in terms of sentimental value. You can tell Pippa from me I'll turn a blind eye if it's returned."

Edna glared at the woman, but Marjorie was grateful she didn't make a scene. Instead, she turned on her heels.

"We're in the sitting room, Marge."

Marjorie wouldn't tolerate employees being accused of theft without proof and would have a word with Christina on the quiet. She watched her and Mary Anne huddling together in hushed conversation as they headed towards the reception room. The rest of the group followed them.

"Thank you so much for today and for going along with my ruse," she said to Faith.

"Anytime, Marjorie, I'm sure you'll explain why when you're ready. I'd better go. Nick's going to take me back to Mum's."

"I'll be in touch," said Marjorie.

Elsa waited until Marjorie closed the door before saying, "Horace is also in the sitting room, plus the police."

"Good," she replied. "Please see to our guests for a while, would you?" Frederick had agreed to keep everyone together in the reception room until Marjorie had spoken to DI Crow. She put her battle face on, determined not to allow that man to bully her.

Horace stood when she entered the sitting room. "Tea, Marjorie?"

"Yes, please."

She noticed DI Crow scowling, but Maria appeared relaxed.

"If you could get to the point, Lady Marjorie. We have work to do," the inspector snapped.

"First, tell me where you are up to with your investigations."

"You might be a member of the aristocracy, Lady Marjorie, but I don't answer to you." DI Crow's droopy jowls swayed up and down while he tried to set his enormous jaw.

"I apologise, Inspector. Of course you don't. We just want to help you get to the bottom of this murder and assert my housekeeper's innocence. I assume you have found out by now that it was she who prepared lunch for Marcus Singleton?" Marjorie sat down, accepting a cup of tea from Horace.

"We know the woman's innocent," Crow replied. "What we don't know is whether you are." His fiery eyes met hers. Her laughter must have appeared rude to the DI, but she was so relieved at hearing the police didn't suspect

Gina any longer. The thought of her murdering anyone was ludicrous.

"He's serious, Marjorie," said Edna. "Apparently Marcus had his own flask the other morning, so none of the staff filled it, but Elsa says it was in the study where anyone could have tampered with it—"

"*Your* study, Lady Marjorie," Crow interrupted. "You've all been lying to us from the beginning. I assume to protect your reputation rather than your housekeeper."

His scorn brought Marjorie out of her hysteria.

"Inspector Crow, we may have got off on the wrong foot, and I'm sorry if we have misled you, but I'm not the person you're looking for. I assume you've heard about what happened to Edna and Christina last night. You can't think I'm responsible for any of that."

The DI's face reddened.

"Mr Tyler and Mrs Parkinton have told us about their illegitimate searches of your guests' rooms today and about their find in Mr Cartwright's room," Maria changed the subject.

DI Crow scoffed. "God save us from amateurs and time wasters."

"If you didn't kill Marcus Singleton, perhaps you could tell us who you think did," Maria continued.

"Now Gina's in the clear, the evidence points to Elmur Cartwright, doesn't it?" Marjorie replied thoughtfully.

"Although I'm not convinced it's him. Did you find anything useful in the briefcase Horace retrieved?" She looked at the DI. "Which we didn't interfere with."

Maria grinned. "Nothing much. It was quite odd. We expected to find all sorts of business documents or valuables and while there was a folder containing contracts, it was stuffed full of A4 printouts of paintings along with a list."

Marjorie rubbed her cheek. "We're back to art again. What was the list?"

"As far as we could see, it's the names of the paintings, artist, price paid, although some of those were blank, and their current value."

Marjorie almost dropped her cup and saucer in her hurry to put them down on the table. "Of course! It's been staring me in the face all along." She jumped up.

A bemused DI Crow snapped, "Is this another one of your subterfuges, Lady Marjorie?"

Edna glared at him. "If you want to find your killer, listen to her. She might be doddery, but her mind's as sharp as a razor. When Marjorie says she's on to something, she usually is."

"Thank you, Edna," said Marjorie. "Although I'm not at all doddery."

"Come on then, Marjorie, put us out of our misery. Who did it?" Horace said.

"We just need to put the final pieces of the jigsaw in place. I suggest we go next door and that the Inspector questions Elmur about his plans to steal one of my paintings and Bruce about his acting as a go-between for art sales to his girlfriend in Budapest. It's time to catch a killer."

Chapter 30

DI Crow was almost grinning as they walked next door, making Marjorie suspect he was sharper than he had made out. She held Horace back and whispered some instructions before she followed the others. Horace disappeared in the direction of the kitchen.

Silence descended when Marjorie and Edna walked into the room with the police. Colm was the first to speak, laughing nervously.

"Who have you come to arrest?"

"All in good time," said DI Crow, playing along. "Please. All of you take a seat while Sergeant Ouloupis and Lady Marjorie ask some questions."

Heads shot towards Marjorie; no doubt the guests were surprised that she should be involved at all. Frederick offered her a smile of support.

Maria began, getting straight to the point. "Mr Cartwright, we found some items in your room which suggest you were about to steal one of Lady Marjorie's paintings."

Elmur's face reddened. His hands trembled while fiddling with his tie.

"What evidence? And what gave you the right to search rooms without a warrant?" Bruce snapped.

"They had my permission." Marjorie thought another white lie under the circumstances wouldn't be out of place. "As the homeowner, I was within my rights."

Bruce thrust his hands in his pockets. "Well, I want it known I object to people going through my things."

"I believe the sergeant's question was directed towards Elmur," said Marjorie, unflinching.

Elmur rubbed his forehead so hard he was likely to leave a bruise. "I told him I wouldn't do it, but he threatened me."

"Who threatened you?" Maria asked.

"That blasted Marcus Singleton. He wanted another painting for his stupid collection and said if I took it, he'd give my firm the contract."

Elmur put his head in his hands when the others let out gasps.

"Please continue, Mr Cartwright," said Maria.

"He told me if I didn't help him, he'd ruin me. I've run up a lot of debt. I er... er..."

"So, you agreed," said Marjorie softly.

Elmur nodded.

"But rather than go through with your plan, you poisoned him." DI Crow's direct question got the desired response. Elmur's head shot up.

"No. No. I didn't kill anyone."

"We also found this book in your room." Maria held up *A Brief History of Poisons*.

Elmur's dark blue eyes bulged as he looked at the book in Maria's hand. "That's not mine. I've never seen it before."

Bruce jumped in. "What are you trying to pull here, Inspector? How do we know you found that in Elmur's room at all?"

"And why are you so interested in Mr Cartwright's innocence, Mr Melville? What do you have to hide?" the DI challenged.

Bruce stared at Crow. "Nothing. We're friends, that's all, and I don't like people nosing through our stuff."

"Did Bruce know about your deal with Marcus, Elmur?" Marjorie asked.

"You don't have to tell these people anything," Bruce snapped.

"This is a murder inquiry," said DI Crow. "I suggest you cooperate or be charged with obstruction."

Elmur wouldn't meet Bruce's eyes, but groaned. "I told him about it when we were at the market. He seemed to understand. Believe me, Marjorie, I didn't want to take anything. I've made such a mess of things."

"So what if I knew about it?" said Bruce. "And if the painting had been stolen, I would have gone to the police, but it wasn't and Singleton's dead. Problem solved, so other than his murder, no crime has been committed here."

Marjorie wanted to tear the arrogant and ruthless Bruce Melville to shreds, but she knew he was right. Nothing had been stolen and Elmur would be afraid to incriminate him any further. Unless she could somehow provoke a confession, there was nothing more to achieve on that line of inquiry.

"How do you think you would have got away with stealing the painting?" Maria asked.

Elmur looked sheepishly towards Marjorie. "Marcus had a plan. He said I should hand it to him through the study window on the night of his death. He was going to leave a lot of muddy footprints in the garden with oversized boots and make it look like a burglary."

"I see," said Marjorie. "And we would find it missing in the morning and call the police while you were in bed, I suppose?"

Elmur nodded.

"Except in the light of his history which Christina has informed us of, Marcus would have made sure someone was framed for the crime – most likely you, Elmur."

"As intriguing as this would-be theft is, I'd like to get back to the murder," said DI Crow, looking at Elmur once more. "During that meeting with Singleton on the morning of his death, you saw his flask. This man was going to ruin your life one way or another, because blackmailers never stop, so you took the opportunity to poison him."

"No! I tell you, I didn't kill the man."

"Well, if Mr Cartwright didn't kill Mr Singleton, who did? Over to you, Lady Marjorie." Maria scanned the room with her eyes.

"That's been the most troublesome question to answer because they each have a motive. Any of them could have added the cyanide to Marcus's flask that morning and the tonic water would have disguised the taste. Elmur's motive we already know. But I believe him when he says he didn't kill the man. Colm's motive is weak. Whilst he may have wanted to keep his affair hidden from his wife…"

Colm flushed a little, but shook his head.

"… he'll be found out one day, and I don't think he would kill to protect the secret. Bruce Melville, although we can't prove it, fences stolen art, but that isn't much of a motive…"

Bruce opened his mouth to protest, but closed it again.

"… he's an opportunist and very careful. I don't believe he would resort to murder to muscle in on the art theft, although I believe he would have swayed Elmur with what he had told him."

Elmur wrung his hands while Bruce glared at him. Neither man spoke.

"Which leaves us with Christina and Mary Anne. Christina has a powerful motive for wanting Marcus Singleton dead…" Marjorie held up a hand to hush Christina, "… but we found her injured in my garden last night."

"Well, it wasn't me," shouted Mary Anne. "Why would I kill him?"

"Why indeed?" said Marjorie. "I overheard you this morning telling Christina you were once married to him. You had no reason to murder your ex-husband, except to get the lucrative contract my son is offering. How desperate are you for that contract?"

Mary Anne's eyes narrowed. "Not that desperate."

DI Crow appeared baffled as Marjorie went to the door and invited Horace in. Horace nodded to Marjorie and

Hercules followed him, looking around the room. He gave Crow a brief warning growl before heading straight to one of the guests. His low guttural growl ensured they didn't move.

"Your killer, Inspector, is the one with the strongest motive, and the most obvious. She has tried hard to cover her tracks, but made a few too many mistakes along the way. Sometimes you can be over-clever."

"I don't know what she's talking about." Christina's eyes pleaded with the DI. "Get this dog away from me."

"Please continue, Lady Marjorie." Inspector Crow smiled.

"For a start, her drunkenness in a roomful of strangers seemed out of character for such a controlled businesswoman. Frederick did his research, as I'm sure you have, Inspector. She's a ruthless CEO who always gets what she wants. I don't believe she would risk her reputation or make such an exhibition of herself unless something more important was at stake.

"I've been mulling over Marcus's death all day long and concluded it had to be premeditated. One of these people had to bring potassium cyanide with them. Christina pretended she didn't know who Marcus was until she got here."

"I didn't," she said, eyes darting back and forth.

"I don't believe you. Christina Makepeace came here with one thing on her mind. She would kill the man who was responsible for her losing her son. The genuine part of her act last night was the anger she felt towards Marcus, who she believes – and she is most likely right – stole a painting from a previous employer and framed her son for it. This anger is coupled with the remorse she feels at abandoning the boy to his fate because she wasn't prepared to accept the damage to her reputation."

"But why tell us about it and risk incriminating herself?" Mary Anne asked.

"Because she knew the police would do their background checks and find out what had happened in the past. She didn't want to risk becoming chief suspect, so she ruled herself out by ruling herself in, as it were. I suspect she and Marcus had conversations before this week where she pretended she was interested in art, and Marcus couldn't resist bragging about his collection. Christina uses her maiden name for business, so he wouldn't have made the connection between her and his previous fall guy. The only decent thing Marcus did for her son Raymond was ask his employer not to prosecute."

"Only to benefit himself," Christina spat the words out, drawing a low growl from Hercules.

"She needed proof that he stole the painting her son was framed for, so under some guise of joint interest, she persuaded him to bring copies of his paintings in his briefcase. Once he showed her those pictures, his killer had the evidence she needed and his fate was sealed."

"This is all very entertaining, but it's beginning to sound like a soap opera to me, and it doesn't explain the book found in Elmur's room. Surely none of you believe any of this?" Christina looked towards Mary Anne, who averted her eyes. "You're forgetting I too was attacked last night."

"I'm coming to that, but first we'll talk about a lost earring."

"What about it?"

"I'll hand this one over to Horace," said Marjorie.

Horace cleared his throat. "I've had a word with Pippa, who's just come on duty—"

"Who the heck's Pippa?" DI Crow interrupted.

"She's the temp who has been serving our meals and cleaning the rooms. This morning, she found Christina coming out of Elmur's room…"

Elmur gave Christina a sharp stare. "You put that book in my room? Why?"

"Let Mr Tyler finish," said Maria.

"… yes, well. Christina came out with a cock and bull story about a lost earring and practically accused Pippa of stealing it. Pippa was so shaken that she forgot about the intrusion into Elmur's room, thinking Christina was looking for the earring, but when I quizzed her just now, she said she thought it was strange. Incidentally, I have the apparently missing piece of jewellery here." Horace held up a pair of diamond earrings.

"How dare you go through my personal possessions?"

"And how dare you plant a book in my room incriminating me in murder?" said Elmur.

"Pippa has identified these. Christina only showed her the one when she offered to continue the search while cleaning the rooms."

Christina was looking more uncomfortable, her left knee bouncing up and down as if it were on a spring.

"And finally, to the apparent attack last night, of which there was only one." Marjorie gave Edna a sympathetic look before staring at Christina. "You were trying to take Marcus's briefcase from my study, placing it on the other side of the window, which you were no doubt about to leave through when you heard someone coming and a knock at the door. After Edna entered, you pushed her over and locked her inside."

Christina gave a mock slow applause. "And then I went outside and attacked myself. This story is getting more unbelievable by the minute."

"You did go outside, but no-one attacked you. Although there was a witness who chased you and you eventually tripped over."

Hercules gave a growl, as if in agreement.

"This is ridiculous. I'm leaving." Christina made to move, but thought better of it when Hercules snarled, baring huge fangs.

"I couldn't work out how one attack – that of Edna – was so clumsy and the other so professional. Christina made out someone touched her neck, and she fainted. That would take the skills of a trained professional at the very least. She made it up, Inspector. In the act of trying to take the briefcase for the second time, she was caught by our four-legged friend here. Not only that, but he growled after her when she left with Horace last night. I mistook it for jealousy because he and Horace had bonded, but it was a genuine dislike of Christina."

"I told you that dog was intelligent," said Edna.

"Why did she want the briefcase?" DI Crow asked.

"Only she can answer that with any accuracy, but I expect it was to make her feel justice had been served."

"Because her son committed suicide, and she was trying to assuage her guilt," DI Crow said, nodding.

Mary Anne's jaw dropped open. "I thought he was alive, but estranged."

Marjorie too hadn't known this, but it made sense. "I expect it's because she can't bear to face up to the fact that she rejected him when he needed her the most."

Christina let out a primeval howl, which shocked even Hercules as he stood guard.

"Do the honours, Sergeant," said DI Crow.

Fifteen minutes later, Jeremy arrived.

"Ah, Jeremy. Just in time for dinner," said Marjorie.

Chapter 31

"I've got to hand it to you, Marge. This one had me going round and round in circles, but you managed to put all the pieces together."

Edna was finishing a full fried breakfast while Jeremy held a much smaller business meeting than he'd expected in Marjorie's study with Colm and Mary Anne. Bruce and Elmur had made themselves scarce, leaving before breakfast, and Melissa, who wasn't part of the business meeting, was having a lie in after all the excitement of the night before. Other than Sally, the temporary staff had been cancelled, but only after Marjorie ensured Jeremy would pay them as per the original agreement.

"It was simple really once we had all the clues in place," Marjorie said, adding, "And thanks to the help of my friends."

"Including the new one."

"Ah, Hercules. I'm going to miss having him around when Sally goes home."

"Have the police got enough evidence to charge Christina?" Horace asked.

"Inspector Crow telephoned earlier to say they had found the key to my study in her handbag and traces of potassium cyanide from the bin in her room. If she doesn't confess, he believes he's got enough to charge her. He sends Edna his regards."

Edna smirked. "I told you. We northerners stick together. He was all right in the end, wasn't he?"

"I admit he wasn't as bad as at the first meeting," said Marjorie.

"I expect the guest list will be reduced to the four of us by the end of today," said Horace. "Jeremy told me he's going to do a deal with the last pair to supply your company."

"It's his, really. I just keep my controlling interest to make sure he – or rather his wife – doesn't spend more than the business can afford."

"Quite right. It's a shame Elmur doesn't have someone like that in his business, poor man," said Frederick.

"I hope he gets his life back together," said Marjorie. She suddenly felt a sense of panic. "You will still stay for Christmas if the guests leave, won't you?"

"Of course we will, Marge. Especially if Sally's cooking." Edna wiped her lips with a napkin.

Horace snorted. "We're looking forward to it. When's the tree arriving? We'll help you decorate it."

"Tomorrow. We must invite Faith and her mother for Christmas dinner."

"I reckon she'd like that," said Horace.

"If we don't have to entertain guests today, do you think we could visit the Christmas market again?" Frederick asked. "I'd like to buy some presents."

"What a good idea," said Marjorie. "It would be lovely to see it without the drama."

"I'll come if you can guarantee no murders," said Horace.

Marjorie chuckled. "I'm not sure I will ever be able to do that."

"I know what I'm going to buy this mutt." Edna nudged Hercules under the table with her foot. He sighed happily.

"What?" Sally asked. She and Elsa had come in to clear away.

"A toothbrush."

Laughter filled the room as Gina came in to help the others. It was lovely to see Sally and Gina getting on so well. There could be no better Christmas present than to find family again. Marjorie thought of her son Jeremy; her friend Rachel Prince, whom she considered the granddaughter she had never had. Looking around the room at her four dear friends, she felt she had the best family in the world.

THE END

Author's Note

Thank you for reading *Murder at the Christmas Market*, the third full novel in the Lady Marjorie Snellthorpe series. If you have enjoyed it, please leave an honest review on any platform you may use.

If you would like to read the prequel to the series, the novella *Death of a Blogger* is available for free when you sign up for my newsletter, where you will receive news and offers once a month. If you prefer not to subscribe to newsletters, the book is available to purchase from most eBook stores, or to borrow, on request, from libraries. Print and audiobook versions are also available.

To find out what happens to our feisty pensioners next, keep an eye on my website at:
www.dawnbrookespublishing.com.

Discover where the Lady Marjorie character began; check out the Rachel Prince Mystery series.

Books by Dawn Brookes

Lady Marjorie Snellthorpe Mysteries

Death of a Blogger (prequel novella)
Murder at the Opera House
Murder in the Highlands
Murder at the Christmas Market
Murder at a Wimbledon Mansion (coming soon)

Rachel Prince Mysteries

A Cruise to Murder
Deadly Cruise
Killer Cruise
Dying to Cruise
A Christmas Cruise Murder
Murderous Cruise Habit
Honeymoon Cruise Murder
A Murder Mystery Cruise
Hazardous Cruise
Captain's Dinner Cruise Murder
Corporate Cruise Murder
Treacherous Cruise Flirtation

Picture Books for Children

Ava & Oliver's Bonfire Night Adventure
Ava & Oliver's Christmas Nativity Adventure
Danny the Caterpillar
Gerry the One-Eared Cat
Suki Seal and the Plastic Ring

Keep in touch:

Sign up for my no-spam newsletter at:
www.dawnbrookespublishing.com

Follow me on Facebook:
www.facebook.com/dawnbrookespublishing/

Follow me on TikTok
tiktok.com/@dawnbrookesauthor

Follow me on YouTube:
www.youtube.com/c/DawnBrookesPublishing

Acknowledgements

Thank you to my scrutiny team for the suggestions and amendments, making the finished version a more polished read. Thanks to Alison Jack for her editing skills and to Alex Davis for proofreading the final document.

Thanks to my immediate circle of friends who are so patient with me when I'm absorbed in my fictional world for your continued support in all my endeavours.

Thank you so much to my Advance Reader Team for comments and support.

About the Author

Award winning author Dawn Brookes is author of the *Rachel Prince Mystery* series, combining a unique blend of murder, cruising and medicine with a touch of romance. She is also author of the Carlos Jacobi crime series and the Lady Marjorie Snellthorpe Mystery series.

Dawn holds an MA in Creative Writing with Distinction and has a 39-year nursing pedigree. She loves to travel and takes regular cruise holidays, which she says are for research purposes! She brings these passions and a love of clean crime to her writing.

The surname of her Rachel Prince protagonist is in honour of her childhood dog, Prince, who used to put his head on her knee while she lost herself in books.

Author of *Hurry up Nurse: memoirs of nurse training in the 1970s* and *Hurry up Nurse 2: London calling*, Dawn worked as a hospital nurse, midwife, district nurse and community matron across her career. Before turning her hand to writing for a living, she had multiple articles published in professional journals and coedited a nursing textbook.

She grew up in Leicester, later moved to London and Berkshire, but now lives in Derbyshire. Dawn holds a Bachelor's degree with Honours and a Master's degree in education. Writing across genres, she also writes for children. Dawn has a passion for nature and loves animals, especially dogs. Animals will continue to feature in her children's books, as she believes caring for animals and nature helps children to become kinder human beings.

.

Printed in Great Britain
by Amazon